I0838713

Their MATCHMAKER

ALLYSON LINDT

USA TODAY BESTSELLING AUTHOR

For my eternal dragon

CHAPTER ONE

Regardless of how much money the participants had, the game never changed; the stakes just got higher. Curiosity made Aaron want to watch the scam in front of him play out, but propriety and the lack of desire to see someone hustled won out.

If Gavin were here, Aaron would probably be distracted enough he wouldn't notice. Fortunately for the group of gentlemen clustered around a woman in a blue dress with a plunging neckline, Aaron's partner was sitting tonight out.

The pack stood near the back of the art gallery. They all wore tailored suits, and the woman in the middle—Aaron was calling her *Ms. Blue* while he observed—held their attention. Except for one man, who spent more time searching the faces of those around him, than trying to catch a glimpse down the front of Ms. Blue's dress. That must be her backup.

"It's a tragic story." Aaron pulled his wallet from his back pocket and plucked out a bill. "I'll give you twenty dollars and two cough drops for the painting. I hate to see a lady in distress."

Her partner snorted. "You're insulting a

mourning woman."

Murmurs of agreement rippled among her pack.

"I'm truly sorry for your loss, miss." Aaron kept the sympathy in his tone. "I feel for your situation, but if the painting isn't worth anything…" If he walked into the middle of the group and proclaimed her a gold-digger, out to steal someone's money, no one would listen. She had them captivated. But if he looked like he was on her side, trying to stop these men from taking advantage of a grieving woman, the hustle would break up, and he and his business partners wouldn't have to deal with it happening on their property.

"This isn't about the worth of the painting." Her partner pushed. To the woman, he said, "You don't need any more grief in your life. I'll give you two thousand, for this unremarkable piece of art."

She choked on her champagne. "How much? For a worthless piece of canvas? But why?"

The mark cut in. "Because he's a cheapskate. I'll give you five thousand."

Aaron feigned shock. "So many generous strangers." He leaned closer to Ms. Blue, and spoke in a stage whisper. "I'd be careful, miss. I believe in charity, but if he's willing to pay you more than a couple of bucks for a worthless painting… perhaps it's worth more than he's saying."

The mark flushed bright red. "Are you implying I'd take advantage of this poor woman?"

"I would never." Aaron kept just as much indignation in his voice. Then he winked at Ms. Blue. "I totally am. I'd get out now, if I were you, before this man tries to steal more than your *priceless* Picasso."

Ms. Blue nodded at Aaron, no longer looking at anyone else. "Thank you." The sweetness vanished from her voice. "Apparently I almost made a terrible mistake."

"Don't mention it." He turned his attention back to the photography exhibition, as the group dispersed. He'd enjoyed watching the hustle as a throwback to his teenage years. However, he was here for the art. It held a kind of joy and innocence the world didn't display in long stretches. A charm that was pleasant to drift into for moments at a time.

A hand on his arm drew his attention. "Aaron Birch." It was Ms. Blue. "I'm Katy. I'd have ditched the loser and low-end hustle, and come learn from you, if I'd known the Four-Billion-Dollar Master would be here tonight."

He hated that nickname. "I don't normally give lessons."

"I can make it worth your time." She traced a finger along the plunging *V* of her dress.

If her version of playful banter was as good as or better than her hustle, he'd see this through, to find out whose bedroom they ended up in. "What kind of conversion rate do I get on that?"

"Excuse me?"

"Is this a penny-per-minute thing? Three-ninety-nine an hour?"

She frowned. "I'm not a whore."

"I never said you were. It's about the back and forth, see? *Worth my time* leads to *conversion rate*, which segues to *value*…" He shook his head. It was no fun if it had to be explained. "I'm sorry, Ms. Blue. I don't think we're on the same page."

"It's Katy. I'm just a little tired. Not paying attention. I get it."

Aaron trailed his gaze around the room, stopping on each face before moving to the next. "We both know you're as much a Ms. Blue as a Katy. Thank you for adding a little spice to my evening, but my date is waiting, and—fair warning—she's the jealous type." And there she was. Or rather, he hoped she'd act like his companion long enough to kill Ms. Blue's interest.

The woman he spotted was spending more time looking at the art than the people. Her glass was still full. She was the least likely to push him away before she had a chance to analyze the situation. It didn't hurt that she was gorgeous—golden hair piled high, with a few ringlets loose around her face; a long, slender neck; and a dress that hugged every inch of curve, without showing a whole lot of skin. Elegant and classy.

He strolled up to her, the clack of heels behind him telling him *Katy* followed. The stranger met his gaze, and he said, "I'm glad you made it, love. I was worried I wouldn't see you tonight."

The stranger wore a half-scowl as she looked between him and Ms. Blue. "Love, this is Katy," he said.

"Cynthia." The blonde extended her hand. She was playing along. Perfect.

Ms. Blue's smile slipped, and she returned the handshake. "Pleasure."
Aaron rested a hand on the small of Cynthia's back,

hoping to strike the balance between looking involved and not pissing the woman off before the gig was up. "My tempting Cyn and I are going to enjoy the rest of the show. Good luck selling your priceless Picasso, Ms. Blue."

*

It wasn't that Cynthia disliked people. They were fine, one at a time. But she preferred numbers. If she added one to one, she got two. Not three, or seven, or a brokenhearted point five. *Two.* She turned to the man who'd adopted her as an accessory. "She owns a Picasso?" Not the most brilliant thing she could have said, but she was piecing together what happened.

"No. But she wants people to think she does. Thank you for saving me, by the way. Aaron."

He was attractive. Dark hair brushed his ears, and he had pale-green eyes she had to tilt her head up to see. It was rare for her to meet a guy taller than her, especially when she wore heels. His suit was made to accentuate and hang from every place a good suit should, showing off broad shoulders and a narrow waist.

"Cynthia. But you already know that." Why was she flustered? She was familiar with his type. They thought they were smooth as shit until someone called them on it, and then they fell apart. Their reaction to someone seeing through their façade was an unknown variable in a world she preferred to keep ordered.

He looked her over, gaze lingering on her

hips and breasts before returning to her face. "And you *are* a sinful temptation."

The cheesy play on her name was enough to snap her reason back on. The attention was flattering, but she knew better than to be sucked in. When she'd started her matchmaking firm, she let guys like this Aaron in the door, along with every other client. Everyone deserved a chance, and she didn't make sweeping assumptions about people.

She'd never been able to match one, though. Guys like him didn't work with her algorithm, because they were so focused on impressing the world, they had no substance of their own. These days she sent them on their way with a smile, an apology, and the assurance they'd have better luck without her computer's interference. "Is that considered an opening line in a place like this?" she asked Aaron.

He raised his brows in question.

"*Hi. I'm Katy, and I own a priceless Picasso.* Is that how the pick-up works here?"

He chuckled—a casual, throaty sound that sent pleasant tingles across her skin in a way she tried to ignore. "Not in the way you're thinking," he said. "It's a hustle."

"Like… *guess which cup the ball is under?*" She couldn't keep the disbelief from her voice. He was comparing high-end art to street tricks.

"Exactly like that, but with a more impressive payout. She finds her way into a gathering like this, usually with a friend to help nudge the crowd, and convinces people she owns said priceless Picasso but has no idea how much it's worth. They believe they underbid her. To them, it's worth twenty million dollars, and they offer her five or ten grand. When they go to pick up the art, she either hands them one of fifty convincing replicas, or more likely, she takes their money and runs."

"That's horrible." She couldn't believe the casual way he said it. "And you let her walk away?"

"She didn't do it yet. And any of those men she was talking to thought they were scamming her, too."

The concept left a bad taste in her mouth. "But still…"

"You think I should call the police? She hasn't done anything wrong this evening." He looked at Cynthia like she was the one not making sense.

She definitely preferred numbers. It was time to wrap this up. "Enjoy the rest of your evening."

"Wait. You're right. It is disturbing. On both their parts."

She should keep walking. So why was she facing him? "You're only saying that because you think it's what I want to hear."

"I'm saying it because I stopped her from doing it. Doesn't matter if everyone in that group was trying to screw everyone else over, it still wasn't right." He quirked his mouth in a smile he probably thought was seductive. It was kind of cute. "If I was saying what I thought you wanted to hear, I'd feed you a line about being one of the owners of this building, ask if you wanted the grand tour, and watch you get flustered again."

"Is giving me a *tour of the building* a euphemism for trying to talk me out of my dress?"

She was making a bit of a leap in logic, that his hitting on her was meant to lead to more. She was bothered that part of her liked his line, though. The notion of being talked out of her dress by this gentleman who knew exactly how to flatter her was more tempting than she wanted.

"You're assuming a lot. What makes you think I don't have a date?" he asked.

She raised her brows in disbelief. "You're here with me. I'm your girlfriend. Isn't that what you told Katy?" Earning her living by hooking people up had taught her a lot of important lessons, number one being that a successful Evening One didn't have to lead to an Evening Two, as long as everyone was on the same page.

"In that case, I don't have to use euphemisms to get you to join me upstairs. You already know how incredible I am, and you're curious to see what we get up to next. You're wondering if we can top how much fun we had at that last place." His smile shifted to something almost challenging.

"Is that what I'm wondering? Considering I struggle to remember the last place… Oh wait—the back room of that place in Chinatown?"

"I love that place. Best dumplings. Do they have a back room?"

This was more fun than she expected. He didn't flinch, and he had a counter at each roadblock. "If neither one of us remembers the back room, it won't be a hard night to top." Despite the derision in her words, she hoped he kept playing along, rather than getting offended.

"We can't have *completely forgettable*. Let

me make it up to you. *That* was the pickup line, if you're keeping track."

"I need to start, if you're going to show me a night I'll remember forever."

His frown caught her off guard. "I don't know. I don't think I'm your type."

He was right, but now seemed like an odd time to point it out. She couldn't hide her curiosity. "What is my type?" According to the program she used to match clients, no one she'd met came close. Not that she would date a client—talk about unethical—but she kept her name in the database for strictly educational purposes.

"Intelligent," he said.

"And that's not you?"

He shook his head. "You don't just want someone who keeps you on your toes with his wit. You want someone who knows the difference between"—he studied her again, this time keeping his attention on her face—"tabs and spaces."

Tabs. Always tabs. "They're two different keys on a keyboard. Mystery solved. I didn't realize you were offering anything long term enough for that to matter." Every time she opened her mouth, she got sucked further into this ridiculous but tantalizing conversation. All she had to do was stop talking and walk away, but no. Something propelled her to say new things.

"I'm not. Does that mean your criteria for letting a random stranger make you moan are different?"

"After that night in Chinatown, my criteria are higher than they used to be." She smiled, to let him know she was still teasing.

"I like it." He dipped his head, and she caught the faint scent of musk. He smelled good too. It wasn't fair. "If you're considering saying *yes*"—his warm breath caressed his skin, and his voice was low—"let's pretend I already talked you into it. There's an office on the fourth floor that's staged for rental, and I'm curious about whether the couch is good for anything besides sitting on."

And there was the arrogance she was looking for. The assumption the conversation would lead to sex. It should bother her more than it did. "Why would I say *yes*?"

"Because you think there's nothing to me but what's on the surface, and the curious bits of you are begging for proof that I'm all talk."

He was perceptive. That probably made a lot of things easier for him. She wouldn't be one of them, despite enjoying the conversation. "In other words, you think I'll go upstairs with you in hopes of being disappointed?"

"I do. And you've set your expectations pretty high."

"You make me sound cynical." Which she was, but it was jarring for someone else to point it out.

"Not at all. Just realistic."

It was time to wrap this up. "Disappoint me before we make it upstairs, and it'll save us both time."

"And how do you propose I do that?"

"If I have to tell you, it's not your idea, is it?" She had no clue what the challenge would get her.

Being unable to second-guess him was exhilarating.

He rested one hand on her hip, thumb tracing tiny circles, and cupped her cheek with the other. When he locked his gaze on hers, her breath jammed in her chest. *Captivating.* He dipped his head, then brushed his lips over hers. The barely-there touch raced through every inch of her, drawing her senses to life.

He stepped back, challenging smirk returning, and cool air mingled with disappointment to take his place. "I'm not interested in talking anyone into an evening they don't want." He grasped her fingers and kissed the tips before releasing her. "Enjoy the rest of the exhibit, my temptation."

She leaned against a nearby wall with a soft *oof* as soon as he was out of sight. What the hell was that?

CHAPTER TWO

Gavin heard the *click* of the front door.

Aaron's voice carried through the house. "Honey, I'm home."

He was in a good mood. Gavin smiled and rolled his eyes. "In the office," he called back. He turned back to his computer long enough to save the search engine spider he was debugging.

"You missed a fantastic gallery opening." Aaron strode toward him, still wearing his tux, bow tie undone and hanging loose around his neck.

It didn't matter how many times Gavin saw him like this; it never stopped being sexy. "You sound like you mean it. What happened to *God, this is going to drag?*"

"I was being melodramatic." Aaron stripped off his jacket as he talked, and draped it over the back of his office chair. "The artwork was stunning. The scenery was better. You should have gone with me."

Gavin wasn't big on social gatherings. Those were Aaron's thing, especially when they had to do with the investment firm Aaron was a partner in. Their agreement was simple—Aaron didn't push Gavin to attend, and Gavin didn't mind if Aaron hooked up while he was there. After dating for more than five years and living together for three, Gavin never worried about the nature of their open relationship. Aaron always came home to him, and frequently had scorching stories to share. When there wasn't a tale for the evening, Aaron improvised. That could get a bit ridiculous, but it was no less fun.

"Did the scenery have a name?" Gavin asked.

"Cyn. With a *C*."

Ridiculous story it was. "Now you're making shit up."

"Nope." Aaron closed the distance between them. "She was witty, intelligent, and honest to God, her name was Cynthia. But it didn't pan out, so I'm about to make shit up."

Gavin shook his head, but he couldn't hide his amusement. "You go out and play all night, while I'm home working, and you think you can come home and tempt me with a raunchy fantasy because you met some hot girl?"

"Hot and intelligent." Aaron leaned over, rested his hands on Gavin's shoulders, and hovered his face less than an inch away. "And your self-righteousness loses its oomph when you've got a raging hard-on." He dragged a finger down Gavin's chest, along his stomach, and over his waist.

Gavin let out a long groan when Aaron gripped his dick through his jeans.

"But I know. You're a gentleman." Aaron made quick work of Gavin's belt, then his button and zipper. "Talk like that isn't appropriate."

When they started dating, Gavin wasn't comfortable with conversations like this. He had exes, male and female, try to trip him up with questions like *do you think they're prettier than me?* When he figured out Aaron not only wanted the truth, but it also turned him on, it only increased Gavin's attraction. "I don't have a problem with it if she doesn't." He struggled to keep his voice even, despite the skilled fingers freeing him from his pants.

"Hmm…" Aaron knelt in front of him, sending a heady shudder through him with each gentle stroke of his shaft. "Say you're working in the shop late one night. Running analysis on some project that's caught your eye. No one's in the office." Aaron trailed his thumb over the head of Gavin's cock with each stroke, pace never increasing. "A call echoes down from reception. You go to investigate, and the woman waiting by the front desk is gorgeous."

"What's she doing there so late?" The fantasy—regardless of how it played out—would be completely implausible. The kind of stuff porn scripts were based on. That didn't stop every word from dialing up his arousal.

Aaron flicked his tongue out and glided it up Gavin's shaft, before resuming the steady attentions with his hand. "She wants to use your phone. She was supposed to meet a boyfriend in a different office, but walked in on him with his secretary. In her frustration, she fled without her purse and can't stand to go back and get it, so she needs to call a friend. As she dials, she shifts her weight to sit on the edge of the desk, and her long coat peeks open at the throat, and along her thigh. You realize she's not wearing much underneath."

Gavin's pulse scored through his veins, burning with the images of the gorgeous mystery woman. He hissed from the sensations of Aaron taking him in his mouth.

"She sees you watching her and hangs up the phone. Maybe you'd like to help her get revenge on the bastard down the hall?" Aaron alternated between sucking and talking, and the words vibrated against Gavin's skin. "It only takes the twist of a few buttons, before she slides her coat off and it tumbles to the ground. You were wrong a moment ago. She's not wearing *anything* under the coat. And damn, she looks good. Round tits, firm and full. Pink nipples standing at attention. You slide your fingers between her legs, and she's already wet. Her mouth opens in a tiny gasp when you touch her, and she says she doesn't want foreplay. She needs you now. Inside her."

"Fuck." Gavin tangled his fingers in Aaron's hair, lost in the visuals and the touch. The story was ludicrous, but the accompanying blow job made all the difference. Intense, raw desire throbbed inside. "I like the sound of that." In a single motion, he nudged Aaron back, stood, and pulled him to his feet. He held Aaron's gaze. "I need to fuck you."

He spun Aaron, so his back was to Gavin's front, jerked his slacks open hard enough the zipper protested, and shoved the clothes to the floor. Aaron's grunts and groans spurred him on. He pressed closer, cock digging into Aaron's back. The familiar scent of aftershave mingled with the faint tingle of sweat, plunged into his thoughts, making him stiffer than he thought possible. He reached around and grabbed Aaron's erection. "I need to drive inside you and pound you till you can't stand." He tugged Aaron's shaft. "And I want you to come hard."

Aaron fumbled with the desk drawer for a second, before grabbing the lube and handing it back. Gavin squeezed a generous amount into his palm. He applied it to his dick, inhaling sharply through his teeth when the cold hit his heated skin, but the temperature balanced quickly. He was grateful their relationship had moved past the needing condoms phase.

He slipped two fingers along Aaron's skin, eliciting an *Oh God* when he teased the entrance and applied more lube. He was done waiting or stringing out a ridiculous fantasy. He thrust inside Aaron hard and fast, past the instinctive clench, burying himself deep inside.

Aaron gripped the edge of the desk until his knuckles paled, his hiss of pleasure mingling with Gavin's grunts.

Gavin set a rapid rhythm, pounding… pushing… losing himself in the tight grip on his dick. With his free hand, Aaron stroked himself. Gavin gripped his hips, digging in his fingers, needing that connection to stay grounded.

As their groans blended and grew in volume, Gavin's head swam. He slammed his pelvis against Aaron's ass. The familiar grabs for breath told him Aaron was close. He didn't know how much longer he could hold out either.

"God, Gavin. *Fuck.* I'm gonna come." Aaron's words were punctuated by gasps. A shudder rolled over his body and tingled through Gavin's fingers, clenching around his cock and squeezing his afire nerve endings.

Now, Gavin could finish. He let go of the reins of restraint, and his balls tightened. The edges of his vision danced and fuzzed, and still he pounded hard and fast. A wave of euphoria nudged his thoughts, and he yielded to it, letting release flood him as he spilled inside Aaron. After he climaxed, he continued to pound until he was spent.

He pulled Aaron upright, back into him, and held him as the haze lightened but didn't vanish. He loved this man. He rested his forehead against Aaron's shoulder. "Welcome home."

Aaron responded with a light chuckle and settled more of his weight against him.

Ten minutes later, both of them cleaned up, they sat in bed next to each other, TV playing and ignored in the background. "Are you going to tell me how the evening actually went?" Gavin asked.

"Same shit, different day. Someone recognized me—a different *someone* than Cyn—and that sucked. Cyn was fun, though."

"Recognized you how?" Gavin didn't want to spoil the mood, but he had to know. It was the one thing they always argued about—where the nickname *The Four Billion Dollar Master* came from. It was a cocky as hell moniker, and for someone who insisted he didn't want to make a big deal out of how they'd made their billions, Aaron didn't do a lot to dissuade its usage. He'd gotten better over the past couple of years, playing down the past and focusing on who they were now. It always stung, though, when the reminder came up.

Aaron scooted closer on the bed and intertwined his fingers with Gavin's. "She knew the nickname but didn't seem to have any details."

"Good." When they pulled it off—selling their first startup for an ungodly sum of cash, six months out of the gate—people clamored to figure out how they'd driven the value so high with a simple contact-tracking app in the early days of smartphones. The last thing Gavin needed was for someone to dig too deep into that sale. The basic details were out there, but they were all attached to Aaron. Gavin wanted to stay as far off the radar as possible.

"And it's not like figuring out what you did then will give her any hints into your past. No one's going to associate the master social engineer with the child star they worshiped in their teens," Aaron said.

"I suppose you're right." Though Gavin wasn't as convinced his past would stay hidden.

CHAPTER THREE

"Cynthia Tremaine," she said to the woman at the front desk. "I have a ten-thirty appointment."

"Of course. Have a seat, and someone will be right with you."

Cynthia took a seat in one of the padded chairs surrounding the glass coffee table in the office lobby.

The lobby looked like so many others she'd seen over the past few months, each intended to show off the bank or investment firm's personality, but looking instead like they'd been copied from a catalog.

"Miss? Mr. Woodhouse will be right with you. He apologizes—he's running a few minutes behind."

Cynthia gave her a practiced smile. "That's fine. Thank you." When she'd started looking for expansion capital for her business, those extra few minutes would have been a grace period to run the highlights of her presentation through her head one more time. To swallow back the nausea and psyche herself up.

After twenty-three *no*'s—she told herself she

wasn't keeping count, but the data never lied—this ritual was habit. Extra time was used to go through her to-do list or simply let her mind wander. Today she was thinking about Aaron. She didn't want to be. The banter, the kiss… It shouldn't get to her. He was better than most at reading her cues, but it wasn't anything to lose sleep over.

That wasn't what gnawed at her, though. Her mind screamed there was something more she needed to notice, and she couldn't figure out what.

She could focus on it later or not at all. She needed her head on straight, for today's meeting. After going through a list of all the banks and investors she could find, who would work with projects like hers, she'd been ready to give up. When this angel investor firm popped up in her search and had time to see her today, she couldn't believe her luck.

They were new, so they didn't have a huge track record, but the one they had was good. Their investments tended to be successful and unique. The firm had a good grasp of technology, and they were willing to take bigger risks if they liked the numbers they saw. In a way, she was grateful it took her so long to discover them. Now she had her ducks in a row, instead of walking in green and new.

"Ms. Tremaine?" A male voice drew her attention. "Jonathan Woodhouse. Sorry to keep you waiting."

Sandy-blond hair, brown eyes, and about her age. Recognition flooded her, and the database in her brain spun, until she found a match. She stood and shook his hand. "It's not an issue. I appreciate you seeing me.”

“Your premise has us intrigued. This way.”

She fell into step beside him. “You were at the exhibit downtown last night?” She hadn’t met him, but she had a good memory for faces.

“The firm owns the property, and the gallery is my wife’s.”

“She’s done an amazing job with this newest artist.” Cynthia was relieved at the chance to break the ice. The stilted small talk that came with these meetings was only one of a list of many things she’d never gotten used to. Today’s appointment would be her one in twenty-three, though, where she finally found the funds she needed and never had to do this again.

“I’ll tell her you said so. Here we are.” He held open the door, so she could step inside the conference room. “We’ve got a couple of our local partners joining us, and some remote from Salt Lake.” He called out the names of the partners on the phone, first, and she was greeted with a chorus of digital *hellos*. She wasn’t paying attention. Her gaze was stalled on Aaron’s face. She should have taken the offer for something to drink after all.

“This is Murdock Birch,” Jonathan said.

Aaron rose to shake her hand. “Pleasure to meet you, Cyn.” His grip was firm and tempting, but the different given name crawled under her skin and soured her fascination.

“Same.” She gave him the same polite smile as everyone else. He might have sunk so low as to lie about something as basic as his name, but that wasn’t a reason to blow her chance with this firm.

They finished the formalities, and she took her spot at the front of the room. This bit was easy. She could shift to autopilot and let her mouth run. "What's The Glass Slipper Theory?" The rehearsed words rolled out without thought. "The practice so many of us engage in that has us waiting for fate to step in and show us the one true love of our life. To give us a sign that some random person is *the one*. A shoe left behind after a surprisingly good dinner. A sleeping princess on a pillar in the forest—not that we see that one too often." Even her chuckle was part of the presentation.

The room laughed with her, and some of the tension in her loosened. "Love isn't so uptight and whimsical, though. Frequently, someone wonderful is waiting next to us—at the bus stop, the coffee shop, or the gym—and we're too busy waiting on *the one*, to see what's in front of our faces. My service takes the fairy godmother out from under fate's control, and gives you direct access to her contact list. Using a series of computer algorithms and face-to-face evaluation, we point clients toward potential matches that are guaranteed to keep them up past midnight. Or for the sake of legalese, at least one matches our unique system provides them will result in three dates. But that takes too much of the whimsy out of things, don't you agree?" Another laugh from her was backed up by the room, and she knew she was nailing this.

Now she just had to keep them intrigued through the less flashy stuff. Like convincing at least one person in the room that they'd make their money back on her service, showing them how she stood out from the standard dating website or matchmaker, with her mix of personal touch and computer logic. She'd struggled to sell this idea in San Jose, because nothing was unique there. Making the drive out here to L.A. might be the change of scenery she needed.

Everyone asked questions, and hope grew inside. She knew better than to get sucked into counting on a *yes* before it happened, but she couldn't help it.

"Excuse me," Aaron said. Or was it *Murdock*? "This Glass Slipper Theory of yours—is it ever metaphorical? As in, someone leaves something emotional behind, rather than a physical object?"

Cynthia's brain ground to a halt on the question. No one had ever gone back to the lead-in that way before. It was meant to be a clever story to prove that type of fairy tale wouldn't get someone anywhere in real life.

"You're being too literal." A woman's voice echoed from the phone. *Liz.*

Cynthia smiled at the speakerphone in gratitude. "Exactly."

"Easy for you to say. You've already found not one, but the two loves of your life, thanks to a random meeting in a bar, a thousand miles from where any of you lives." Aaron's tone was playful.

That was intriguing, borderline unprofessional, and none of Cynthia's business, except that the details helped make her point. "With my service, you could have skipped the long-distance trip, to make that connection."

That brought the conversation back on track,

and she finished answering their questions without further hiccups. She met their gazes one by one, giving each of them a warm smile as she wrapped up her presentation. "I appreciate your time. When would be a good time to follow up with you, for a decision?"

"You've got a fantastic platform," Jonathan said, "but I don't see any longevity in it. It's the kind of offering that runs on novelty, and once that wears off and something flashier replaces it, the product fades into the background."

Once upon a time, that phrase sank into her soul and crushed her hope. Now it was one of several *thanks but no thanks* reasons she heard at the end of a presentation. That didn't stop her from being disappointed. She kept her friendly expression in place. "I understand. Thank you again for your time. I'll let you get back to your day."

She'd spent the last several years of her life building this. It wasn't some noble pursuit, but it was the sum of her adulthood. Everything she had, financially and emotionally, had been poured into this.

That was what she got for turning silly dreams into business plans.

*

When Aaron asked Cyn his questions, he hoped for more of the back and forth they had last night. He would have been disappointed with the lack of exactly that, but her professionalism and pitch impressed him. He was irritated to hear Jonathan's *it's not for me* at the end of the presentation. Not because Aaron thought everyone in the firm had to agree, but it meant Jonathan went into the meeting expecting to turn down the project, and it wasn't fair to stack the odds against an entrepreneur without warning them they were up against that prejudice.

Aaron cringed as one partner after another passed on the deal. This was a sure thing—he felt it—but it would be nice to have backing. He'd made a couple of bad predictions lately, and his own capital wasn't as big a cushion as he'd like. That was okay; he simply needed a win.

"Cynthia, wait a moment if you would," he called as she opened the conference room door to leave.

She paused and turned to face him. The doubt on her face was another reminder of what drew him to her last night. "What can I do for you… *Murdock*, was it?"

"*Aaron* is fine. Murdock looks impressive on the letterhead, but it's not what my friends call me."

"Are we friends?" The corners of her mouth twitched with an unformed smile.

"I'm hoping. I'm also hoping you have five more minutes to talk. We can go in my office or stay here." He'd absorbed everything she had to say about the custom dating service, the hybrid technology, and the hands-on solution. As long as it worked in practice the way it did in theory, he'd found his win.

She studied him for a moment, before pulling out the chair next to him and taking a seat. "My time is yours."

"I was impressed with what I heard. I want to

work with you and fund your project, as long as you're willing to meet my conditions."

He swore her blue eyes lit up. Who knew that was really a thing? Her smile was hesitant but grew as the seconds passed. "Fund… me? Really? Just like that?" Her disbelief combined with excitement was attractive. Not that it mattered if she was about to become a business partner.

"It's not quite that simple. I did say there was a condition."

There was a long pause, and she furrowed her brows, before she said, "Draw up the paperwork. I'll have my attorney look over it. I'm sure we can reach an arrangement we both agree on."

"You may want to get started on this before we sign the paperwork, because my signature doesn't go on there until it's done."

Her smile wavered. "All right. I'll bite. What do I need to do?"

"I want to see your application at work."

"That's fine." She pulled a folder from her bag, enthusiasm returning. "I skimmed over the details for brevity's sake, but I have test cases, beta customers, and a slew of positive data and happy early customers. What can I show you?"

He closed the lid on her folder and slid it back toward her. "I'd like a hands-on demonstration. To experience it for myself. Test cases are fantastic, but firsthand experience trumps everything."

"You want me to find you a date?" she asked.

"Something like that."

She frowned. "The application isn't for everyone. You may be one of those people the process doesn't work for."

"Why not?"

"It's not for serial daters. It's meant more for those people who are looking to settle down. Hence the three-date guarantee."

"You wound me." He clutched his chest with feigned pain. "To be fair, I'm guilty as charged—one point in your favor—but it's for my boyfriend."

She broke into laughter, then stopped when he didn't join in. "You're serious."

"He and I like to experiment, and it would be wonderful if you could set us up with someone whose company we enjoyed for a night."

She gathered her bag and stood. "I'm sorry. I think you misunderstood. This isn't an escort service."

"Wait." He covered her hand, and a shock of heat raced through him. He swallowed the response. "That's not what I'm asking for. It's an unconventional request; I get that. But I genuinely want someone we can take out for an evening and enjoy his or her company. You don't have to oblige, but it's my condition."

She shifted her weight from one foot to the other and furrowed her brow. "That's not what the software is for."

"A relationship like ours isn't for everyone, but we enjoy it. If you're looking to expand your offering to a broader audience in the future, come back to me." He wasn't trying to be cruel. It wasn't about teasing her and then ripping the funding away. In a case like this, he had to cover his own ass. The request served his purposes, but it also proved her product.

She took a step back and put her paperwork back in her bag, but she didn't turn away. She chewed her bottom lip. Seconds ticked away. "All right. I'm in."

He rose and extended his hand. "I'm happy to hear it, Cyn. Let's talk business."

CHAPTER FOUR

Gavin frowned at the unknown number on his cell phone, then hit *Decline*. In his experience, people who blocked their numbers when they called wanted to sell him something, and he wasn't in the mood to tell anyone he wasn't interested. He turned back to his work, searching for the tentative focus he had before the interruption.

He hovered his fingers over the keyboard, willing them to type. Anything.

Nope. Wasn't happening. His computer clock told him it was almost noon. Perfect time for a break. He grabbed his phone again, to send Aaron a text. Before he could, the device chimed with the same message that floated at his fingertips.

You free for lunch? Aaron asked.

Gavin liked that they were on the same wavelength. He sent back a, *When and where?*

Aaron replied with, *The place by the office, in fifteen?*

I'll be there. Gavin needed the break. The zone he'd been in, before the unknown phone call, took him all morning to achieve. Something had him distracted, and until he either shook it off or figured out what it was, he wouldn't get any work done. Hopefully taking an hour or two off, and Aaron's company, would help.

There was no point in driving during the day if he wanted to get anywhere quickly. The downtown L.A. traffic would be a gridlock until late in the evening. Fortunately, they only lived about four blocks from the building Aaron shared with his investment partners.

The sun peeked through the clouds, chasing away the humid chill, but not so hot it scorched. The November rainy season in California was one of his favorite times of the year, and the walk helped him beat back his jumbled thoughts.

Gavin arrived five minutes early and wasn't surprised he was the first there. Aaron was probably just leaving his office.

Gavin found a clear spot of sidewalk near the blank steel support of the building and pulled up his email. An unknown name in his inbox caught his attention. Ignoring calls was one thing, but over email, he could sate his curiosity and find out what a stranger wanted without having to talk to them.

Hi Gavin,

They started out friendly and pretending to know him. Points in their favor. The sarcastic thought flitted through his head.

I've got the opportunity of a lifetime for you, and I'm hoping you have time to meet with me and chat.

That was as generic as a message could get. But for the most part, the grammar and spelling were legible, so Gavin gave them credit for that.

A comeback career for Hollywood's hottest child actor, fifteen years later. You're grown up, sexier than ever,

Gavin deleted the message without finishing it. Acid churned in his stomach, fueled by irritation and bad memories. He learned a long time ago that, whether he gave the overzealous talent-agent of the week a polite *no thank you* or a terse *fuck off*, replying only confirmed they had the right guy.

It wasn't that Gavin had vanished and started life over, with a name change and new identity, when he left acting. He didn't have the skills to take himself that far off the grid or the inclination to hire someone who did. But by putting things in Aaron's name—utilities, mortgage, multi-billion-dollar IPO's—and keeping Gavin's name off social-media accounts, made Gavin as good as invisible unless someone pried. Like an agent who decided they could use a career boost that included a comeback from the heartthrob who dominated teenage Rom Coms in the early part of the century.

Gavin couldn't go back to that life, though. When he got into acting, it had been the only thing he wanted, and he was one of the lucky few who made it, with his killer smile, gorgeous eyes, and a decent job of delivering his lines.

And he loved the lifestyle that went with it. Not the stress so much, but the unchecked debauchery made it easy to ignore that. Until it almost cost him his sanity, to the point of threatening his life.

Aaron saved him back then. Gavin became quick friends with the runaway pulling card tricks behind the studio. Aaron was about the only person Gavin knew who didn't care about the name on the marquee.

Gavin's parents were furious when he wanted to quit acting, but he had enough money to hire a good lawyer. It was like a bad Lifetime movie, but with the implausible bits left in. Gavin got himself emancipated by age sixteen, and as he and Aaron hit their early twenties, their friendship became more.

Five years ago, Gavin thought he'd moved past the addiction problems. He could handle fame, now that he was older. More mature. Had a real support structure behind him. So he agreed to start simple, with a low budget indie film, to ease his way back into the spotlight.

Two days after the movie premiered at Sundance, Aaron found Gavin in a studio rental car, in a parking garage in downtown Salt Lake, staring at the city's premier attraction—a temple. Who the fuck built a city around a temple? At the time, Gavin was trying to figure out if he'd rather go out in a blaze of glory via overdose or via dramatic car ride off the edge of a mountain.

Aaron stayed by his side during detox. The four-billion-dollar tech-startup sale that earned Aaron his nickname was the mental half of Gavin's recovery. Gavin used building the company—the hype around it and its perceived value—as a way to climb out of the pit that drove him to drink. Focusing on that project allowed him to divert his thoughts, until they reordered themselves and he could shrug off the addiction.

"You in there?" Aaron's question pulled

Gavin from the uncomfortable tumble into the past.

Gavin shook the clouds away and gave him a smile. "Yup. Lunch?"

"If you're sure you're all right." Aaron eyed him with concern. "I've been trying to get your attention."

"I'm super-swell." Gavin winced as the catchphrase from his movie days slipped out.

"If you say so." Aaron would know the reassurance was false, but he'd give Gavin time to process before pressing for more.

They made their way inside, were seated a few minutes later, and placed their order.

"How'd things go with the dating-app people?" Gavin was grateful he had a pending topic to change the subject to. Anything that took his mind away from where it had wandered.

"Promising." Aaron's simple response didn't hide the glint in his eyes.

"That's appropriately vague."

A smile slipped through Aaron's neutral demeanor. "I liked it. She needs to provide another piece of proof, and I'm going to buy in."

"Sounds fair. I'm surprised she didn't already have that information."

"She did." Aaron took a sip of his water, then swirled the glass enough to make the ice clink. "But I want to see if she can do something less mainstream with the product. Might as well push the concept to its limits."

He was dragging this out for effect, which worked. Gavin was curious. "Do tell."

"She's going to find us a date."

Gavin shivered, his skin feeling as if Jack Frost breathed down his neck. "*Us?*"

"I'm not going to have all the fun myself."

Gavin clenched his jaw. He didn't care that Aaron hoped to find them a hookup. The two of them frequently brought a third person into their relationship—sometimes for a night, other times for months. It was the details of this particular proposal that set his teeth on edge. "This is the write-up you read to me a few days ago, isn't it? The one where she boasts that her computer takes all sorts of personal information, stores it, and matches it against a database of other clients?"

"That's the one." Aaron's glee slipped. "What about it?"

"Well, an agent emailed me this morning. Which means I'm back on someone's radar. At the risk of sounding like a selfish asshole, I'd rather tone down my digital presence, not give a slew of identifying details to a random stranger, to keep on file."

Aaron's expression softened. "I know. I promise I took that into consideration. But really? Someone found you again so soon?"

"Yes." Gavin was probably making a big deal of nothing, but caution kept him sane. "You thought about the consequences?" He wanted the conversation back on track, so they could get it out of the way more quickly and move on.

"The process is one-hundred percent anonymous. She's got an extensive non-disclosure agreement around all client information, and that includes us."

"And if she decides selling my name to the tabloids is a good reason to break that?" Gavin was being paranoid, but it was with good reason. He'd had a doctor's office, a barista, and several hotel clerks do exactly that in the past.

"First of all, she loses her funding if she does that." Aaron's tone was sympathetic but practical. "I can't imagine the paparazzi will pay her enough to make up for what she can get from the firm. Second, with a service like hers, if word gets out she's done that, she loses half the clients in L.A. And third, I trust her. Are sure you're all right? The email you mentioned is what has you spacing out and on edge, isn't it?"

"Yeah." Gavin sighed. Aaron was right. All of those were good reasons this arrangement was probably all right. "I don't know why, but the past hit me hard today."

"You were up late, watching *Where are they now?* reruns, weren't you?" Aaron teased.

"Or reliving someone else's episodes in my dreams." Gavin forced himself to chuckle, and it helped lift some of his stress. He had to admit the idea of how the system worked intrigued him. And if he was being rational, it held a lot less risk of someone recognizing him than picking up a random stranger at the bar did, because they would only meet the person they matched with.

"I can tell her *never mind*," Aaron said. "It's my condition for funding, not hers. She'd be happy to take it off the table. I guarantee."

Gavin shook his head. "Don't do that. I'm in. Let's see how this thing works." The functionality fascinated him. His hobby was figuring out if people were predictable enough that computer algorithms could second-guess them, and this was right up his alley.

He just had to quiet the nagging discomfort inside, instead of letting it swell the way it was now.

CHAPTER FIVE

Cynthia approached Aaron and his boyfriend in the lobby of the office she shared with several other startups.

Aaron looked good, the same as every time she saw him. He wore those expensive suits as if he were created for the cover of GQ, and it seemed like amusement always danced in his eyes. Whether or not he was the serial dater she assumed he was; he was sexy. Not that it mattered. She'd never been big on *happily ever after* for herself. There was no romance or fairytale in an emotion that could be predicted by a computer program.

That didn't stop her from wishing for a moment that she were the client instead of the agent in this arrangement. She wouldn't mind hooking up with these two for a night.

The man with Aaron was just as compelling. The dirty-blond hair that flopped over one eye was almost status quo for this town, but his brown eyes held a captivating warmth and mystery she struggled to look away from. He was tall and lanky, looking like he'd be more at ease in a faded T-shirt and jeans than in his button-down and tie.

And he was familiar. Eerily so. She scanned his face against her mental list of everyone she knew, but didn't find a match. This was going to drive her nuts.

"Aaron." She pasted on her professional mask and extended her hand. "Glad you could make it."

He stood and shook her hand. His grip was firm and his skin warm against her palm. "I think you're just saying that, but I'm hoping to make it true. This is my partner, Gavin."

The name ticked something in her head too, but she still couldn't grasp it. "Pleasure to meet you."

"Same." Gavin kept his hands in his pockets, but the way he traveled his gaze over her sent goosebumps rising along her entire body. He met her gaze and gave her a smile. "Thank you for indulging us."

"The pleasure is all mine." Was there a hidden meaning in that? No. She was grateful for the chance to land an investor. Nothing more.

She led them to her office, going over the highlights of what she'd already told Aaron with Gavin. She had been tweaking the inputs for the match process all day, so it would accept data from two sources instead of one. It was days like these when she wished she hadn't pushed her best friend, Emily, out of her life. It wasn't the biggest reason she missed Em, but working on this process without her was a reminder that they lost a good friendship.

Cynthia was infamous for saying the wrong thing at the wrong time and being too stubborn to take it back, but she'd tried this time—called Emily several times, to apologize. Emily never returned those calls.

Cynthia pushed the past aside and gestured for Aaron and Gavin to take the seats across from her desk, while she took her own chair. "I need to ask you some questions," she said. Might as well dive into the professional aspect of things immediately, rather than dwelling on the fact she had two gorgeous men in her office, who wanted her to find them some company to share for the evening. "Normally I'd ask you separately, so you don't contaminate each other's data with your answers. This time, since the point is to match you both with the same person, I'll let you play off each other."

Clothed. Not clothed. Somewhere in between. Images assaulted her of what that *play* might involve. What was wrong with her today? She never let clients distract her like this. It was probably her brain rebelling, because she knew how critical this match-up was to her business.

"Things like what our favorite color is?" Gavin asked teasingly. "Turquoise, for the record. And I don't care for long walks on the beach. Not here anyway. I hear the ocean is nice in Australia, though. Coffee for breakfast, toast dry—those kinds of questions?"

She appreciated the break in tension. "Sort of, but not quite. This isn't like a Cosmo dating quiz. It's a little more like word association. Some of my questions are very specific. For instance, would you rather stay up all night and sleep in, or go to bed early and get a start on the day before the rest of the world?"

"Stay up all night," Gavin said at the same time Aaron answered, "Get up early."

That ought to make things interesting. "Noted. Other questions are more freeform, and intentionally vague. I'd like you to answer the first thing that pops into your head. Like what's your favorite toy?"

Aaron smirked. "The handcuffs in the top drawer."

"Aww, that's a good one." Gavin huffed in exaggerated disappointment. "I was going to say my vibrating game controller, but I like his answer better. Can I change mine?"

Maybe letting them bounce their answers off each other wasn't a good idea. Cynthia couldn't help but smile at the exchange, though. "No. First answer is final."

"What are the odds that, when we're done, you'll explain your logic to me?" Gavin leaned in and rested his forearms on the desk.

She studied his face, looking for a hint he was joking. No one cared how the data worked. That was boring stuff. Only sincerity stared back. She shook her head. "Sorry. Some of this is proprietary. Secret blend of eleven bits and bytes, and all that."

"If you're only using eleven, I'm impressed." Aaron winked.

"It's all about quality, not quantity." She turned back to her computer. "Are you ready to get started?" For the next half-hour or so, she ran through her current questionnaire, doing her best to keep a straight face through the teasing and bad jokes. She'd never had this kind of trouble staying professional during an interview before.

The words stuck in her throat when she realized where she was in the questions, and she mentally shoved the hesitation aside with enough force that it rattled in her skull. "The next block is about sex." She was impressed she kept her voice steady. Which was ridiculous. She never had a problem with this before. She could be clinical, because sexual preferences were as much a part of the job as whether someone liked country or heavy metal.

There was no reason to turn into a giggling school girl over two men. She repeated the reminder until it stuck. Just because she knew Aaron was an enticing kisser and she was fighting off fantasies about being pressed between him and Gavin—heat flowing between all three of them, hands sliding anywhere and everywhere—didn't mean she would lose her cool.

"Like the other questions, these may seem random, though not as much. But I promise it's all between us, except for whatever you decide to share with your date." She added a chuckle at the end. That was all part of her script, and if she could stick to that, she'd be fine.

"But this is a dating service. Not an escort service." Gavin still watched her with that intense curiosity that stole her breath and fuzzed her thoughts.

Fortunately, this was part of the script as well. "That's true. I never assume where the dates will or won't lead. Everything outside of me hooking you up and hoping you enjoy each other's company is incidental and between the three of you. For instance, the two of you are looking for…"

"Scintillating conversation. That's it. Everything else is incidental." Aaron winked.

"Right." She let her skepticism bleed into her reply. "So we start with the easy questions, and probably the most obvious. But I make no assumptions, so you have to answer them all. Are you abstinent and/or waiting until after you're married to have sex?"

Aaron snorted. "Really?"

"No assumptions." She was enjoying this more than she should be.

"Do you want details about the *no, we're not abstinent*?" Gavin asked.

She did. Vivid, intense, details. *Enough.* "We'll get to those later in the process. I'm just going to put *no*."

"Do you get into things like what attracts us first to a person? Favorite physical features?" Gavin looked to be taking this more seriously than Aaron.

Cynthia liked that someone was actually interested in how this worked. She had to be careful, or she'd geek out and start talking tech with Gavin, instead of doing her job. "No. I ask about body type, but nothing more specific than that."

"Why not?" Gavin wanted to know.

"Because the number of people who are honest about it is so low, it's not a valid question."

"In other words," Aaron said, "you expect most people will say, *it's what's on the inside that counts*, and you don't buy it."

She shrugged. "Experience is a cruel

mistress. Are you ready to move forward?"

"Can't wait." Aaron's tone was enthusiastic.

She read from the screen. "Your favorite dating accessory." This was one of her most vague questions, because it was the best way to lead a conversation a lot of people were uncomfortable diving into head first.

"Necktie." Aaron didn't hesitate.

"Worn around the neck?" Cynthia prodded, hoping he'd open up more. For clinical purposes, of course. Not because the single word danced over her like flames licking her senses.

"If it's worn somewhere else, it ceases to be a *dating* accessory." Aaron twisted his mouth. "Worn around the wrists. Not mine."

"Or over the eyes," Gavin added.

The responses summoned accompanying fantasies in Cynthia's mind, and she bit the inside of her cheek to keep fantasy from rushing in. "I guess it's a good thing there are two of you, then." *Don't flirt with the clients.*

"Not the first time we've heard that." Gavin's expression shifted from serious toward playful, but the intensity in his dark eyes didn't vanish.

This was a dangerous way to let this conversation meander. Cynthia didn't have the desire to reel them back in, though. "Why a necktie? Is it the texture?" The question had nothing to do with her form, and everything to do with the images teasing her.

"Convenience," Aaron said.

Gavin nodded. "It's all about spontaneity."

"I don't know what kind of men you date"—

Aaron held her gaze—"but I don't typically wear a rope as an accessory."

"Though I suppose I could find an excuse in a pinch." Gavin added.

Aaron scrunched his face up in mock-thought. "Pinching has its place too."

"If we're just throwing logic to the wind, ass-slapping is one of my favorite accessories." Gavin grinned.

She should argue that it wasn't wearable, but thought of handprints on bare skin danced in her mind, and she didn't know if she could pretend to be professional if she let one of them describe that in detail. "Sensation play, then?" She struggled to turn the conversation back to the form.

Gavin furrowed his brows. "*Play* sounds so formal. You wouldn't think a word like that could be anything except fun, but you tack *play* on the end of something sexual, and suddenly it carries an expectation."

"Which is bad because… spontaneity?" Cynthia warred between falling into vivid conversation and doing her job.

"It's not always bad," Aaron said. "It has its place."

Gavin looked around her office. "This place, for instance, has a lot of potential for play."

"I think we're getting off track." Who was she kidding? She didn't want to get back on track. She was fascinated with the way Aaron and Gavin fed each other in conversation, and wondered if they did the same thing when it came to sex. Which intensified the throb between her thighs.

Aaron studied her. "Are we? You never mix business with pleasure?"

God, she wanted to. "Never."

"So you're not enjoying this?" Gavin gave her an exaggerated pout.

"Maybe a little." Her heart slammed into her ribs as she let the confession slip out.

"What would it take to make it a lot?" Aaron prodded.

"Nope. We're going back to the questions." Despite the words, she was about to do exactly what she said she wouldn't, and mix business with pleasure. "What kind of potential do you see in a room like this?" As long as they kept everything verbal, she could convince part of herself that this was professional. And save any tidbits shared for tonight, when she was home alone with her vibrator.

CHAPTER SIX

Gavin was grateful he let Aaron talk him into this, if for no other reason than the interview was fun. Cynthia kept up with them, never missing a beat, and the way she pushed to hide her flustered blush was alluring. "You're so clinical." He kept the teasing in his voice. "We're talking about the potential of your office. That's work-related, isn't it? Your desk for instance. It's mostly clear. The simple, obvious answer for where you'd start, play-wise, is on that."

"You mean your date," Cynthia corrected him.

He studied her. "Do I?"

"Sure. He means the vague, generic *you*," Aaron said. "If that makes you comfortable. But he's wrong. The desk is clean because you're a neat freak, and you might get distracted if something gets knocked off."

Gavin waited for her to point out that was a very specific statement for something intended to be about a vague, generic person.

Despite the pink flushing Cynthia's cheeks, she smirked. "Gavin did say the desk was an obvious answer. So is the couch, if you were going there next."

Gavin glanced at the sofa behind him, then turned back to her. She had captivating eyes, and they sparkled with amusement. "Not the couch." He shook his head. "One of the leather chairs by the table. Exposed metal arms and legs. Perfect for binding you to."

Cynthia shifted in her seat.

Were they making her squirm? Fuck, he hoped so. He wouldn't mind making this scenario real, to find out how wet she was.

What were the odds they could take her out or take her here, rather than go through this ridiculous investor contract? Probably pretty slim, since there was still a business angle to this for both her and Aaron. That didn't stop Gavin from enjoying the exchange, and he had zero intention of dialing it back if no one was protesting.

"You've only got two neckties between you," Cynthia pointed out. "I'm having trouble with the math—comparing those to the four total limbs that need binding."

Which meant she'd surrendered all movement. Gavin's cock strained against his zipper.

"Then I hope you wore a dress or a skirt. Preferably with thigh-high stockings, like you wore at the exhibit." Aaron's voice held a heavy current that Gavin recognized instinctively. Aaron was as turned on as Gavin.

Cynthia ducked her head. "I wasn't wearing—"

"You were. Thigh-high stockings, and a dress slit high and showing off the hint of lace, but only if you shifted your weight right," Aaron said.

This kept getting better. Gavin picked up the thread. "That solves the issue of not-enough accessories. Your stockings bind your ankles, ties on your wrists, and—oh no—your skirt is pushed up over your hips, leaving you exposed."

"Oh no, indeed." Cynthia drifted her fingers along the edge of her collar, bottom lip caught between her teeth. She wasn't making any pretense of typing now. Her other hand vanished under the desk.

Gavin was tempted to slide his hand between her legs. Or work his cock free while she fingered herself. He could go either way.

"And if you're in something like you wore the other night, tied at the back of the neck and leaving your back bare, it's easy to untie the straps and let the dress fall away." Aaron's voice dropped an octave.

Maybe they should give Cynthia a break. Which was an excuse. If Gavin kept this up, he was going to need an outlet sooner rather than later. "How does something like this get categorized on your questionnaire?"

Cynthia fiddled with the button on her blouse. A flick of the wrist, and it would slip from its hole, giving a better glimpse of her full breasts underneath. Already her quick breathing made them strain against her top. "Medium propensity toward bondage, higher on the exhibitionism and voyeurism scales."

"I don't think programming has ever sounded so sexy." Aaron winked. "How do you put in the details of what comes next?"

She traced her fingers along her skin, dipping between her breasts then back up. Did she realize she was doing that? "I guess it depends on what *next* is."

Aaron rose from his seat a few inches, then sat back down, gripping the arms of the chair hard enough his knuckles turned pale. "Standing behind you. Kissing along the back of your neck. Cupping your exposed breasts. There's some of the pinching that we mentioned earlier. How hard is up to you."

"So, low to medium on the sensation and pain scale." Cynthia's voice was strained.

Apparently trying to dial things back to clinical didn't make a difference. Need slid along Gavin's skin, prickling his nerve endings until the slightest movement of fabric amplified his arousal. "Closer to medium. Expect marks."

"Noted." Cynthia's voice cracked.

So much for staying removed. Fuck it, with pretenses. "While Aaron's giving your upper half attention, I'm kissing along those long, exposed legs and over your thighs.

Cynthia whimpered, blush spreading to her neck when Aaron raised his brows.

Gavin didn't flinch. "Sliding a finger inside you. Licking along your slit. Enjoying the way you squirm."

"*Oh.*" Cynthia's exclamation didn't have that growing pleasure sound Gavin expected. "I know where I know you from." She clapped her hand over her mouth, her eyes wide. "Or rather… squirming and marks?"

Gavin's mood soured, as ice flowed into his

veins.

"You've never seen him before, unless it was grocery shopping or getting coffee." Aaron shook his head. The sexual tension evaporated from the room, leaving suffocating reality in its place.

"You're Gavin Jackson from—"

"Do you have all the data you need?" Gavin had known this was a possibility, but the jarring transition made it difficult to process.

"Yes." Cynthia seemed to shrink in her seat. "It is you, isn't it? I had the biggest crush on you when I was in junior high."

Normally that single phrase was enough to spoil Gavin's day. This evening, it almost brought his mood back to even-keel. "If I tell you *yes*, you're not allowed to put that in my profile. We signed an NDA."

Cynthia frowned. "You think… I wouldn't ever. I'm curious. It's not often I get a face wrong. But *anonymous* means exactly that."

The assurance didn't ease Gavin's mind completely, but it helped. "How long until we get results?"

"A minute or two. At least for initial feedback. It's going to be a larger list than your final output, until I filter it by people who are willing to surrender the three-date guarantee and are interested in dating more than one guy at once. That's not data I have stored for anyone else."

"Perfect." Aaron's cheer sounded forced. "We're helping you improve your business model. This is going to be a fantastic partnership."

Gavin used Aaron's words to smother his

disappointment at the abrupt interruption. It was a good reminder he and Aaron were in this for fun, but not with the woman behind the desk.

*

Cynthia had never been fond of her knack for saying the most inappropriate thing at the worst possible time. Today she wasn't sure if she was grateful for the slip-up or not. She'd been enjoying the *interview* a lot more than she should, but now she couldn't stop thinking about the possibilities they presented.

For some other lucky guy or gal.

Even if she did want to slide her fingers between her legs and take care of the nagging ache. Maybe once Gavin and Aaron left.

She pushed the thoughts aside and turned back to enter their information while it was fresh in her mind. Some of the inputs stayed blank, thanks to their rambling conversation, but she was able to fill in most of the data the computerized side of things required.

She hit *Execute*, to let the program do its work, and waited for it to return a large list of names. She needed to put more filters in place before it would be effective, but this way she could make sure the system was accepting two inputs correctly.

Her computer chimed, indicating there were results. One set went to the client inbox, and the other to hers.

She stared in disbelief at the screen.

Matches Found: 1

Cynthia Tremaine

Fuck. She must have programmed something wrong. Her information was only in the system for testing, and it never returned as a match unless she entered off-the-wall data.

"Is everything all right?" Aaron asked.

"Yeah. Fine." She deleted the match results on her end, and sent them to the trash for the men's profile. "I'm ironing out some glitches, as I mentioned. I may need a day or two before we can move to the next step."

Gavin's chair scraped back, teetering on two legs before deciding not to fall, when he stood. "Great. Drop Aaron an email when it's done."

"I appreciate this." Aaron gave her an apologetic smile. "I look forward to building our partnership."

"Me too. I'll be in touch." She saw them to the front door and shook their hands. It was no use trying to ignore the firm grips that had her bound in her imagination.

She turned away, despite the temptation to watch Aaron and Gavin stroll to the elevators.

"Ms. Tremaine. This came in for you, while you were in your meeting." The receptionist handed her a FedEx envelope.

"Thanks." Cynthia grabbed it and tore off the strip as she wandered back to her office. Her thoughts were on the last hour or so, as she sank into her chair. She should be figuring out why her algorithms were off, but nope. She was pondering the logistics of being tied to one of her office chairs.

She tilted the envelope and slid out the

contents, only half-paying attention to what was inside.

Notice to cease and desist.

The words caught her eye, and fantasy flew out the window. She gave the notice her full attention. Law firm letterhead. Official looking legalese. And once she filtered through the wordy explanation, a notice that she needed to immediately stop development and sale of her dating app until she could prove she wasn't using any intellectual property from Emily.

Cynthia frowned. It never should have come to this. Emily was her best friend.

Until Cynthia had to choose between Emily and Paul, her own brother. Cynthia tried to repair the friendship but didn't get anywhere. She didn't think this dispute would actually happen, though.

She couldn't afford a legal dispute to prove this app was hers, and the buyout amount listed in the letter was ludicrous. She dialed Emily's number, knowing what she'd hear, even before the phone connected.

We're sorry. The number you have reached has been disconnected.

Cynthia blew a puff of air, to knock a strand of hair from her face. Next, she dialed the number on the notice. After several minutes and various transfers, someone answered who was familiar with the case.

"I'm looking to get in touch with the person who filed this order," Cynthia said.

"It doesn't work that way." The man—Ryan? Brian? She hadn't quite caught his name—sounded cool and emotionless. "Once you've spoken with your attorney, we expect a reply stating your intentions."

"But if I could just talk to Ms. Lowry—"

"You'll need to do that on your own dime, so to speak. Client information is confidential. I can't stop you from contacting her outside of this firm, but I wouldn't recommend it, and I certainly won't give you her number."

Cynthia sank back in her chair. That made sense, but she had hoped… "I see. Thank you for your time." She disconnected before he could reply.

She wasn't giving up this company. She'd put too much work into it, to walk away now. Once she found Emily they'd make things right. The question was, could she do that before the cease and desist required her response? It had been six months she and Emily spoke, so the odds didn't seem good, but Cynthia wouldn't have held on this long if she wasn't capable of a little optimism.

CHAPTER SEVEN

Aaron rolled over in bed and reached out. When his hand met an empty spot of cold sheet where Gavin should be, he frowned and opened his eyes. The clock said it was barely six in the morning. Gavin hated being up this early.

There were a half-dozen reasonable causes for his side of the bed being empty, but that didn't stop uneasiness from settling over Aaron. He pulled on some clothes and wandered through the house, looking for his other half. The tap of a keyboard filtered toward him, as he neared the office. Aaron turned in that direction and paused in the doorway.

Gavin sat in front of his computer, his fingers flying over the keys, multiple windows open onscreen. Displayed in front of him was a series of photos, what looked like articles, and code.

"Morning," Aaron said. "You been up long?"

Gavin didn't look up.

Aaron crossed the room and rested a hand on Gavin's shoulder.

Gavin jumped and whirled in his seat. It took him a moment to focus his bloodshot eyes on Aaron. He blinked and shook his head. "Jesus. Give a guy some warning."

"What's going on?" Aaron's concern grew with each passing second.

Stress lined Gavin's forehead, and his screen was littered with tabloid websites. He switched to a different web browser window and scrolled to the top of the page. It took Aaron about two seconds of scanning, to get the gist of the post.

Which Hollywood Darling is Making a Comeback?

Fucking clickbait headlines.

The text of the article was brief.

Child actor turned heartthrob, Gavin Jackson, was seen leaving the offices of The Brunson Agency. Sources say talks to revive his career are in progress.

The accompanying images and captions were damning. Photos of Gavin, as clear as if the photographer had posed him, taken at various locations around the city, and labeled in each case. In concept, it wouldn't be hard to capture him on film—it wasn't as though Gavin was a recluse—but it meant the photographer knew who he was and where to find him.

Several of the pictures included Aaron, as the two left the building Cyn's office was in.

The building labeled as the home of The Brunson Agency.

The email Gavin got the other day wasn't such a big deal. Those came in from time to time. But this was too specific. Too close to home. Aaron clenched his jaw until his teeth ground together. It wasn't the same as Gavin rebooting his acting career, and it didn't mean he'd slide into old habits. However, he didn't look like he was in the best frame of mind, and that was enough to make this troublesome.

"Did you call Don?" Aaron asked. Don Twents was their lawyer, and always had takedown notices on hand for scares like this. Except there hadn't been anything this specific in… ever.

"Yeah. But it's not that simple. The story went viral, and I can't find the original source. There are a series of top sites that picked it up within a few minutes of each other, but there's no originating point."

"Does it matter, as long as it goes away?"

"Yes, it matters." Gavin clenched his fist and sighed. "Sorry. It's just that… when was the last time someone besides the DMV took that clear and distinctly unflattering picture of me? And with your picture out there, you're going to be a lot easier to track down. You lead to me, our home address gets out. I'm trying not to blow this out of proportion, but we have to consider the consequences."

"We've always known this was a possibility." The words sounded more reassuring in Aaron's head than spoken aloud. "But we'll deal with this. The last thing I want to see is you falling back into that pit."

Gavin gave him a weak smile "We're nowhere near that point. I promise."

"Good. Have you slept at all?"

"Not really. The alert came in around one, and I got sucked down the rabbit hole of following links."

"Go sleep. Let Don deal with this." Aaron spun the chair so Gavin faced the door. "And I'll change the terms of investment with Cynthia, so we don't have to go back to her building."

"You need a win at work, and she may have a good product."

Aaron looked at him in disbelief. "But that doesn't mean we need her to set us up. You're sleep deprived for sure, if you think that's a good way to stay off the radar."

"You're right. Do what you need, but don't cut her loose because of me." Gavin stood and gave Aaron a quick kiss before ambling from the room.

Aaron sank into the now-empty seat and stared at the pictures on the screen. It shouldn't be a big deal. The paparazzi got images of everyone all the time. It was a consequence of having any kind of celebrity. That didn't stop concern from snaking through Aaron.

* * * *

Cynthia tried to put the *cease and desist* out of her mind overnight, but when she got to her office the next morning, it sat on her desk, looking deceptively banal.

She shoved it aside and sat in front of her computer, to get to work. She had more coding to do, but today she also had a full meeting docket. After her system made the automated match recommendations, she got to the personalized part of her service—working with her clients face to face, to go over their match options and narrow the list using their input. She met with clients, brought lists back together, and assembled final matches from there.

Each time she pulled up a new task, her gaze drifted back to the legal paperwork. She shoved it under a stack of folders, but she knew it was there, almost as if it whispered her name from beneath its paper tomb.

If she could get in touch with Emily—if she could make things right...

Why was Cynthia so unyielding the last time they talked? She regretted it as it was, but this was another wound. She tried emailing Emily before, to no avail, but that didn't stop her from sending off another note.

Emily,

I know I screwed up, and I just want to apologize. Please?

Cynthia

Not that she expected it to go anywhere. None of their other friends seemed to have Emily's current cell-phone number, and her parents weren't giving up the information. Not that Cynthia blamed them.

She pulled the C&D out and stared at it. The dollar amount Emily wanted in order to relinquish her intellectual property mocked Cynthia. Emily had earned something, and it would be nice to have her as a partner, but that option was off the table.

If Cynthia secured an investment through Aaron, could she make the numbers work? Not up front, but the lawyers would work on a payment schedule, wouldn't they? She wasn't going to ask unless she could make the numbers work.

Several hours later, the math almost added up. Not quite, but it was close. Hope flickered inside. None of it would matter if Aaron didn't agree to work with her, though.

Which meant working hard to find matches for him and Gavin. She'd never worked with *find the same date for two of us* before, but the steps to allow for it were in place.

She had to fix the back-end code, to return matches other than herself, then call existing clients to see if they were interested in an arrangement like dating two men already in a relationship.

Step One took longer than she expected. It was almost eleven that night when she shut off her office computer and dragged herself out to her car. She had her list, though.

In the morning, she arrived at work psyched up and ready to start calling clients. She had several questions for them, rather than asking out of the blue, "Would you consider dating two men at once?"

She met a wide-variety of responses when she got to that part of her questionnaire, ranging from *Are you kidding? That sounds hot*, to *What the fuck is wrong with you? Why would I do that?*

She was grateful when the process was over. Her nerves felt like they'd been forced through a cheese grater. This had to work. *Please.* She dialed Aaron, the short prayer repeating in her head.

"Murdoch Birch." The name and the stress in his voice caught her off-guard.

She grasped her wits quickly. "Hi. This is Cynthia Tremaine. Is now a good time?"

His sigh echoed off the receiver. "Sure. What

can I do for you?" His tone shifted toward pleasant but still held an edge.

"I've got preliminary results for you." She pushed ahead. Second-guessing his mood and whether it had to do with her would only stall her. "When can I get the two of you back in the office, to move to the next step?" The thought of being face to face with Gavin and Aaron again sparked inside, sending heat racing over her skin.

"I don't know if we can make that appointment. Now's not a good time. I don't mean this moment; I mean in general."

Were the exhaustion and irritation directed at her? She couldn't have him pull out. Not now. Not without a chance to prove herself. "I'm flexible. I can meet in the evening, the weekend—whenever. Even if we need to put it off for a week or two. Please?" She clenched her jaw shut before she could slide into begging.

"Are you able to meet us at home?" His tone softened.

As a general rule, she preferred not to. It wasn't only for personal safety. Her office was a neutral environment, and that impacted how people answered her questions. She was making plenty of exceptions for Aaron. Would one more matter? Especially considering that the neutral environment didn't seem to inhibit the men last time. "I can do that. Fair warning—environment can taint the results."

"I'll keep that in mind. Privacy is more important. I have the utmost faith in you, and if for some reason you feel the setting hurts the process,

I'll take it into consideration."

Her heart hammered hard. She needed to keep this encounter on track, unlike last time. Knowing that didn't erase the visuals the men stuck in her head. If this weren't a business arrangement, she'd agree in an instant to be trapped between the two. "What evening works best for you?"

"Tonight, if you're free."

Great. Not a lot of time to bring herself under control, but also less freaking out about whether or not this would go her way. *Think positive.* "Sounds perfect. In the meantime, I'm adding your matches to your account inbox. Both of you should look them over before then, if you can, and see if anyone stands out to you."

"Sounds fantastic. I'll email you the address, and we'll see you at seven."

As Cynthia disconnected, the flames rolling over her skin faded but didn't vanish. Concern about the C&D warred with Aaron and Gavin's voices etched into her memory as they discussed the best way to tie her to one of her own chairs.

She just had to make it through tonight. As long as things went right, Aaron and Gavin would have their matches, and Cynthia would be a hair away from being financed and putting the sexy men out of her mind.

CHAPTER EIGHT

Cyn's coming by tonight, to discuss matches. I'm swamped with work. If you have a chance, will you look through our dating profile inbox and vet the candidates, for anyone who catches your eye?

Gavin smiled when he read Aaron's email, and sent back a quick, *I'm on it.*

It wasn't so much that he was looking forward to seeing who Cynthia's system paired them with, though he was curious. It was more that he wanted to spend several hours digging through the details and guessing at how she made the process work.

He opened the site and navigated to their inbox. The (1) in the trash can caught his attention, and he clicked. His smile grew when he saw the contents. *Isn't that interesting?* She'd wait until last.

He sifted through names, details, images, and preferences. There had to be things Cynthia was taking into consideration on the back end that she didn't display on the site. Not all of the questions she'd asked were reflected here. No matter how many angles he hit the details from, he couldn't make sense of how she did it.

A new text chimed on Gavin's phone, and he grabbed the device. He stared at the time in surprise. How was it almost seven? He read the message from Aaron.

Running late. Entertain Cyn until I get there?

Gavin typed, *Entertain? Is that open to interpretation?*

As long as you share the details after.

Gavin smirked. He wouldn't jeopardize Aaron's business prospects that way, regardless of how tempting Cynthia was. Gavin felt even stronger about that now. She had a brilliant mind, and from everything he saw, she deserved this opportunity.

A few minutes later, someone rang the doorbell.

Gavin greeted Cynthia at the door. She wore a slacks-and-jacket suit that tapered down her figure, highlighting every curve without being revealing. It sent his imagination racing. Her hair was pulled up tight. *Gorgeous.* Though he wouldn't mind finding out how she looked with the clothes strewn on the floor and her blond locks loose and mussed.

"Aaron's running late and sends his apologies." Gavin stepped aside and opened the door wider. "You're welcome to reschedule or come back, but if you've got an extra hour, you can hang out here."

She chewed her bottom lip and furrowed her brow, then stepped inside. "My night is open. I can stick around."

He gestured to the living room. "Can I get you anything to drink?"

"Water would be great. I don't do alcohol

while I'm working." She perched on the edge of an easy chair, her back straight, ankles crossed, and knees pressed together.

Water was fine with him. He was more at ease when the temptation wasn't there. He grabbed her drink and returned seconds later to find her still sitting like she had a rod running up her spine, a smile pasted in place. That wouldn't do.

He handed her the glass and sat across from her.

She never broke eye contact. "I'm glad it's not as hot as last week."

Nope. Wouldn't do at all. Gavin didn't blame her for the small talk, but he was looking for a more in-depth conversation. If he could break the ice fast, maybe Cynthia would relax. "I'm not," he said.

"You like it hot?"

"And sticky. The kind of searing that leaves you breathless." He ginned when she raised her brows. "Oh. You're talking about the weather, aren't you?"

"I am. Are you always *on*?" She continued to study him as if she wasn't sure what she was supposed to do next, but her posture relaxed, and she sat back in the chair.

"It depends on the company I'm keeping."

She almost smiled. "If I were a younger me, fresh out of college and looking to brag about my psychology degree, I'd analyze that statement."

The media's brand of pop-psychology had been the bane of his existence when he was younger. He pushed back the jolt of distaste that rose in his throat. "But because you're not?"

"I'm not arrogant enough to do that. Helping you pick a date is a different universe than gauging what makes you tick."

This was better. She looked comfortable, and it was the segue he wanted. "Is that why you started your company? A fascination with human psychology?"

"The Glass Slipper Theory is—"

"I don't want the sales pitch." It only took a few words for him to know he was about to hear something memorized. "I assume it was good enough to sell Aaron. I want your story."

"You really don't. It's a bit silly and not super flashy."

"That sounds like life in general." Certainly like Gavin's private life, as opposed to what the media made of him. "I don't care if it started with a lemonade stand and grew to your first broken heart when the partnership fell apart. I want to hear it."

"It's not even that inspiring." When she laughed, her eyes crinkled at the corners and pink dotted her cheeks. A blush of amusement. "The sales pitch tells the whole story, but in a prettier wrapper. The reality is thanks to a series of… debates I had with my best friend in college." The shadow of a frown crossed her face. It vanished so quickly he might have imagined it. "The result was that I said love was a set of emotions that could be controlled, driven, and directed. It was predictable. She called me a cynic. I told her I'd prove it."

"*Ouch*. Cold. How do you go from that to matchmaking?" Gavin might agree if he didn't have Aaron. There was something magical there. "And she had a point. It sounds a tad cynical."

"More than a tad." Cynthia's amusement was back. "One-hundred percent and then some. I'm not that kind of jaded anymore, though I'm still a make-your-own-fate kind of person. She and I are data geeks, so we tuned it into something more. We used it to set up friends. Messy business—never set up friends. You have to choose sides after."

"I'll keep that in mind."

"But when it worked, it was as good as fairytale magic. That's me selling the product, by the way."

"I like it." He did. It took a little while to pull out her playfulness, but not as much as he'd feared.

She ducked her head and tucked a strand of hair behind her ear. "Anyway. One day I realized I'd spent so much time on it, I should start getting paid for my work. So I spun it into an actual thing."

He was torn between the urge to dig more into the details of her tech and the desire to push the light mood a little further. Before he could decide, the front door latched open.

A moment later, Aaron joined them. "So sorry I'm late." Tension coated his words. He loosened his tie and dropped on the couch next to Gavin. "Did I miss anything?"

"Your partner was forcing me to admit I'm bitter and jaded." Cynthia teased.

"There was coercion but no force." Gavin held her gaze. "Not unless you beg first."

Her blush darkened.

"Actually"—Gavin looked at Aaron—"we were discussing how, if it weren't for you, Cynthia would be my long-lost soul mate." Mostly, he tossed the *soul mate* comment out to throw Cynthia off. It wasn't quite a conscious thing, though he recognized it as soon as the words passed his lips. More a habit born of years of keeping people at bay. It was also a good way to stash the temptation to keep flirting with her—push it over the top.

"Should I be worried?" Aaron didn't look worried. Instead, some of the lines of stress etched around his face faded.

"She's a self-professed data geek. Uses analysis to keep her world making sense."

Aaron glanced at her. "That is kind of sexy." He had a similar tendency toward distracting conversation, but his was born from being a street hustler in his early years. It was part of the reason He and Gavin played off each other so well. Their tangents tended in the same direction.

If Cynthia wanted to use that psychology degree, she'd have a field day with them.

"Should we get started?" Her suddenly sharp tone indicated Gavin had struck his mark in dialing back the conversation.

With a second glance he realized she didn't appear upset. Her lips were swollen and flushed, and her irises wide. The same expression she wore the other night in her office. That was tempting.

Aaron looked between the two of them, brow furrowed. "Ready if you are."

*

When Cyn called Aaron earlier, he was ready

to tell her the deal was off. The investment, the terms—all of it. Gavin was part of the reason. Aaron was also feeling gun shy on the investment front. He'd spent his morning dealing with a hardware startup on the brink of bankruptcy. They'd made a number of mistakes, and their company value had dropped to zero almost overnight. He wouldn't be able to recoup the losses.

Gavin was right; Aaron needed a win. The firm was barely two years old, and Aaron would burn through his capital more slowly if he lit it on fire. It was the one problem he always had when he played the bullshit game. He could spot a lie a mile away, in the dark, filtered through earmuffs, but if the person telling the story believed it, he got sucked in almost every time. And in this industry, most people believed in what they were doing. They'd never beat the odds if they didn't.

When Cynthia said *please*, though. Aaron couldn't tell her *no*. And when he walked into the house tonight, to Gavin's laughing face and Cyn's embarrassed smile, his doubt bled away. Even when she shifted to her cool, professional mask, something pleasant lay underneath, and Gavin was still happy.

Aaron might not decide to go through with the deal with the dating app, but for now, he'd made the right choice.

"Did you both have a chance to look over the matches saved to your inbox?" Cynthia asked.

"Yes," Gavin said.

Aaron took a seat next to Gavin on the couch. "But I trust whatever he has to say."

Cynthia raised her brows.

"Does that have the potential to taint the results too?" Aaron asked.

"New territory here." Cynthia opened her tablet case and tapped on the screen. "If you're both okay with that, so am I."

That was an open-ended answer, compared to how defined her criteria had been so far. It made Aaron even more curious to see how this went.

They made their way down the list of nine names—a nice assortment of men and women. Cynthia would ask if Gavin was interested, and each time, he'd say, "I don't think so."

The process took less than ten minutes.

"Should I not have asked you to do this?" Aaron asked him.

"You should have. But that's not the entire list."

"It is." Frustration leaked into Cynthia's words. "Are you willing to go for a Round Two?"

Gavin shook his head. "We're not done. Cinderella hasn't tried on the glass slipper yet."

"I don't know what you're talking about." Cynthia's denial was sharp, and she studied her hands as she spoke.

"Then you didn't delete your own profile from our match list?"

That was interesting. Aaron was definitely right to ask Gavin to look at the matches. Not that Aaron should consider even for a moment that Cyn was a viable match, if she was going to be a business partner. Lust warred with reason inside, arguing it was just one date, and it was part of the contract. *No.*

"What if we pick you?" Gavin asked.

Aaron tried to force out an objection, but the words stuck in his throat.

"That's not an option." Cynthia's voice wavered.

"Then why are you in the system?" Gavin asked.

"My name's in there for testing. Like a one-person control group."

"It's just for dinner. That's the deal, right?" Gavin's argument echoed Aaron's thoughts too closely.

"We were going to order in anyway." Aaron bit the inside of his cheek. *Bad. Wrong.* The problem was he didn't want to take it back. This was a conflict of interest. *It's just for dinner.* That was a pretty good counter. And realistically, if they got along with Cynthia, it meant her algorithms worked, and there was something to her app. That was the point.

"It's only a valid match if both parties agree to see each other," Cynthia said. "That's part of the process. The only reason I'm here."

"You're going to leave before the food shows up?" Gavin was pushing this hard.

Aaron couldn't deny he'd like a few hours with Cynthia that weren't business related. "If you stay, just through the meal, I'll call my side of the agreement done. But only if you would have taken the date if this wasn't a business arrangement."

Cyn studied him, mouth twisted in a frown. Silence stretched through the room. The air conditioner kicked on, loud in the stillness, as if to point out maybe this wasn't a hold-your-breath-worthy event.

CHAPTER NINE

A *yes* lingered on the tip of Cynthia's tongue. It struggled to push its way out, while she argued with herself. This was a business. Dating the clients, even if it was only one meal, was unprofessional.

It wasn't as though she put herself on their list. The system picked her as a valid option. If match-her and business-her were two different people, match-her would take the date with Gavin and Aaron, and business-her would legitimately secure funding. Both hers liked the way that worked out.

She mentally shook her head, to rattle some sense back into place. The last thing she needed was to add more confusion to this mix, by thinking of herself in two-person terms.

Was she working the system, or making a legitimate deal? She didn't have the right kind of ego to assume that intentionally putting her name on their list was a sure-fire path to success.

Gavin leaned in and rested his elbows on his knees. "The other night, you said the system makes the match but what comes next is up to the people involved."

She was flattered he was pushing the issue. "I

did. But this is different. I control the system."

"Which means even if you put your own name on the list, you'd have to be doing your job, looking for those characteristics that make matches click, to know I'd nibble. Don't worry, no full-on biting unless you beg." Gavin winked.

Damn him, for vocalizing half her argument, and for sending a flush of heat racing over her with a few simple words.

"If it helps with your decision," Aaron said, "take yourself out the equation for the night. Check Cynthia the entrepreneur at the door. Be the woman who picked our names out of the dozen or so you were matched with. Detach the evening from your in-office life."

Double damn. Aaron spoke directly to her *what if.*

Gavin studied her. "Unless you're not interested."

"That's definitely not the issue." She snapped her jaw shut, to stop more words from slipping out before she could consider them. *Screw it.* If she was going to enjoy their company, it would be as much on her terms as theirs.

Besides, she was here, and it was only dinner. It had nothing to do with the fantasies that danced in her thoughts thanks to their last encounter. "I guess I'm missing the point of my own pitch, if I walk away from the opportunity in favor of waiting for fate to drop something in my lap."

"Exactly," Aaron said.

Gavin smirked. "Then it's settled. You're staying."

* * * *

Cynthia moved back into the living room with the men. Dinner was a lot of fun, though the conversation was thinner than she expected. It took all of two minutes to discuss how long they'd each lived in L.A., and she didn't dare ask about Gavin's famous past, after the reaction she got last time.

The lack of substantial conversation would make it easier to call it an early night. She could ignore the disappointment dancing inside that the evening was exactly as discussed.

She stopped in front of the chair she'd occupied before.

"You can't sit over there, all isolated and aloof." Playful teasing lined Gavin's words. He grabbed her wrist and tugged her toward the sofa instead.

A thrum of electricity sped over her skin. "I can't squish between you."

Aaron positioned himself on the couch so it appeared that was exactly what he intended. "Why not?"

Because that could complicate things. Remind her she wouldn't mind a more intimate end to the evening if business weren't involved. "I have onion breath."

"Then you should have picked them off your pizza." Gavin sat and pulled her down between him and Aaron, so her thigh pressed against Gavin's.

Cozy and comfortable. "That seems a bit wasteful."

"Besides, we ate the same thing you did." Aaron shifted so his knee rested against hers, and settled his arm behind her back. "Either you have a real reason or not, but no excuses."

She laughed. "Fair enough. I'm sitting, aren't I?"

Gavin nudged her with his shoulder. "Are we good enough friends now that I can pick your brain about how your software works?"

"Buying me pizza doesn't mean you get my trade secrets. I hope my friendship is worth more than that, too." Cynthia kept her tone light. Playful. It was easy to sink into this and forget the outside world for a moment.

"It was a good pizza," Aaron said.

She rolled her eyes and shook her head but couldn't hide her smile.

"It's not about the pizza, it's about what came with it," Gavin said.

"Or who?" Aaron smirked. "Never mind. That's too obvious. Too easy."

"I am not." Cynthia tried to force indignation into her voice, but her laugh disrupted it.

"Nope, you're not." Gavin trailed a finger down her arm. "That's part of the fun. Is that a *no* on the trade secrets?"

She struggled to believe anyone but her would find those details interesting, but reason said, if she could get sucked into it, someone else could as well. "I'm not sure what kind of information you're looking for, but I might-could be persuaded."

"I like the idea of persuasion." Gavin's voice dropped an octave, sending delicious chills down

Cynthia's spine.

"I don't think you've got the same thing in mind as I do." She forced her voice to remain steady, despite the vivid images that splashed across her thoughts—of him pressing closer, backing her into Aaron… She shook the thoughts aside.

"But you're not certain." Aaron's tone was as coaxing as Gavin's was playful and seductive.

"I hate to assume." She looked at Gavin. "You're welcome to take a look at the code if you want, after the investment contract is signed."

Aaron cleared his throat. "But you hate to assume."

"I'm optimistic. Otherwise I would have given up about twenty pitches before I got to your firm." This was better than the dinner conversation. She enjoyed the way each tangent flowed into the next and then back again. The tantalizing thoughts teasing her senses.

"The secret's not all in the code, though." And Gavin was back on the original topic.

Definitely fun. "No. I purchase aggregate data from a variety of companies. Compiling what they have *is* part of the code, though."

"Does that include figuring out that someone who likes Oreos also enjoys having their ass slapped?"

Her cheeks heated, and the images in her mind intensified. Bending at the waist to kiss Gavin, bare butt in the air. Aaron's hand landed flat first on one cheek, and then the other. "That's a touch oversimplified, but yes. If person ninety-two does or likes certain things, they're more likely to be into another, seemingly unrelated set of things. I have access to millions of numbers, so it makes it easier to guesstimate."

Aaron placed a finger under her chin and drew her face toward his. It was a bit like watching a tennis match, but with more anticipation dancing through her veins. "I'm curious. Does your profile say you like Oreos?" Aaron asked.

Cynthia didn't have to reach far, to figure out what he was actually asking. Reason told her to shut this down. A simple *no* would do. But she was being someone else for the night, right? And searing flames spilling over her and igniting her nerve endings didn't want to settle for time alone later with her vibrator. "It does."

"I'd ask if it's the cream filling that does it for you, but that feels crude." Gavin's breath was hot on the back of her neck.

She wanted to lean into the sensation. Let his fingertips follow a similar path. She resisted. "I don't get the impression that holds you back very often."

A smile tugged at the corners of Aaron's mouth. "Be fair. Blatant innuendo is different from a crude joke."

"Sometimes." Gavin's voice was barely a whisper, but she felt it over every inch of her body. "But really, I'm wondering—are you interested in being the filling in a sandwich cookie? I'm hoping for *yes*."

So was Cynthia, along with the wide range of promises that went with it. "Yes."

Gavin pulled out the chopsticks holding back her hair, and it tumbled loose around her shoulders.

She turned to him. He dragged his gaze over her face, then brushed a finger over her cheek before tucking a strand of hair behind her ear. "Better." He didn't pull his hand away.

Her voice caught, but she pushed through it. "Is this where you tell me I look prettier this way?" she teased.

"I let your hair down because it makes it easier to do this." He knotted his fingers in her hair and tugged her head.

A jolt traveled through her scalp. She gasped involuntarily, and her nipples strained against her bra. Behind her, Aaron let out a low groan.

Gavin hovered his lips millimeters from hers. "You're breathtaking regardless." He brushed a kiss along her bottom lip, then nipped the tender skin.

Her pulse tore through her veins, and her restraint snapped. She pressed in close, crushing her mouth to his. Aaron kissed along the back of her neck, down to where it met her shoulder.

Gavin swallowed her whimper. He pulled back to meet her gaze. His eyes shone with lust and laughter. "First time as the filling?"

"Yes." She didn't have an issue with casual sex. It was the best way for her to get laid, her being a cynic about romance and refusing to get tied into a relationship full of empty promises. But her experiences were relatively tame. "That doesn't mean you need to be gentle."

Aaron caught her earlobe between his teeth and tugged. "Glad to hear it." A growl cut through his words.

Desire grew in her gut and traveled lower, to

throb between her thighs. Gavin kissed her again, hard and hungrily. She grabbed his shirt in her fists. She was desperate for something to ground her. It didn't do the trick, and she didn't care. Since she was someone else for the night, she'd dive in head first and enjoy every minute of it.

Aaron glided his fingers under her shirt and over her bare stomach. She was torn between pressing against Gavin, feeling every inch of him, and leaving space for Aaron to move.

When Aaron worked up the front of her blouse, undoing the buttons one at a time, her decision was made. She let go of Gavin, to let Aaron drag her jacket and top down arms, leaving her in her bra. She needed more—the sensation of skin on skin—but she didn't want this to be over too quickly.

Gavin slipped a finger under one strap on her shoulder and slid down toward her breast. He pulled the lace away, barely touching her nipple. She hissed and arched her back, to get closer, but he kept enough distance to tease.

Wetness pooled between her legs. Each time she shifted her weight, the seam of her slacks dug into her, taunting but not providing relief. She grabbed the hem of Gavin's shirt and yanked it over his head.

"Anxious?" he asked.

She gave a strained chuckle. "Very."

"Good." He scooted back, breaking all contact.

The cushions shifted, and Aaron stood. He extended his hand, and when she took it, pulled her to her feet. He looked her over, and need followed everywhere his gaze traveled. "What was it you said that first night we met?" he asked. "That you were prepared to be disappointed?"

It figured that it would come back to bite her in the ass. "I don't think those were my exact words."

"Your meaning, though." Aaron didn't sound upset. "That's all right. I don't intend to live down to that expectation."

"That's a big promise." She forced bravado into her voice.

His smile grew devilish, as if he knew she was about to sell her soul, and that they both looked forward to it. "I'm not worried about it."

She swallowed the mewl that rose in her throat.

"The couch is good for making out, but there's more space in the bedroom to play." Gavin joined them and settled a hand at the small of her back. He pointed her toward the hallway and gripped her waist. "But first, take off the rest of your clothes."

"I—" Her vocabulary chose that moment to abandon her.

Aaron stepped in front of her. "It's a simple command." He undid the button on her pants and pulled down the zipper, then shoved her slacks and panties to pool around her feet.

"Bra next." Gavin's lips vibrated against her shoulder.

She reached behind her to undo the clasps, and let the lingerie fall to the ground. Anticipation and desire stole her reason. Being exposed like this was both terrifying and freeing.

Aaron drew a line along the middle of her chest, under one breast, and up to her nipple. He pinched the swollen nub and rolled it between his fingers. The sting of pain was enticing. He increased the pressure as he claimed her mouth.

Gavin slid his hand between her legs, teasing her entrance. "You're soaked." He scraped his teeth along the skin where her neck met her shoulder. "Enjoying things?"

She moaned in response, not able to speak with Aaron's tongue dancing around hers. If this was just the introduction, she might not survive the rest of the night. It could be the best way ever to go, though.

Gavin drew his finger—slick with her juices—back to nudge her other hole. She gasped at the penetration, though he didn't move too deep.

Still tweaking her nipple, Aaron used his other hand to part her folds and zero in on her clit. The new touch against her swollen sex pushed her toward climax. The air stole from her head. She pumped her hips against Aaron, trying to get closer. Seeking release.

Orgasm built inside, pushing her breaths out in short gasps for air. She closed her eyes, falling into the combination of touches and letting sensations run together until they focused on a single point near Aaron's attentions.

Then every touch vanished. Before she could process what it meant, Gavin smacked her ass. The loud slap tore her eyes open, and the sharp feeling of his palm against her skin made her press her legs together.

"Bedroom. Now," He growled against her ear. "I need to fuck you, and I'm not the only one."

CHAPTER TEN

Gavin was so hard his balls ached and his cock dug into his jeans. When he stripped off his jeans, his dick sprung free of its prison but didn't find relief in the open air. The right conversation with Aaron was its own kind of foreplay, but adding Cynthia to the mix brought a new level of temptation.

He was grateful he didn't have to choose which of them to study. Aaron had shed his clothes as well, and stood behind Cynthia. She was curves and seduction. He was sculpted and delicious. Aaron pulled two condoms from the dresser and handed one over her shoulder.

She intercepted it before Gavin could grab it. "May I?" Her tone wasn't deferent, but more playfully submissive.

He raised his brows. "Sure."

She ripped the foil. When she rolled the rubber on, her touch was light, and he jerked against her palm. He wrapped his hand around hers, to tighten her grip on his shaft, and guided her to stroke. It would be easy to let Cynthia finish him this way, but he wanted to be inside her.

Gavin dropped back onto the bed, and pulled

her toward him. "I want to watch you ride me," he said.

Her smirk was impish, as she straddled his legs. She hovered over him, her heat near enough to feel, but not touch. He nudged her opening with the head of his cock, then thrust up.

Her cry when he pushed inside her was musical, and her pussy wrapped around him, squeezing tight.

Behind her, Aaron kissed along her neck, and reached around to cup her breasts. Gavin didn't know which he liked more—the feeling of Cynthia, slick and wet around him, or the sight of Aaron making her gasp with each new pinch and caress.

Cynthia rocked against Gavin.

He had to dig his fingers into her hips to slow her down. "You'll make me come," he warned.

She caught her bottom lip between her teeth. "I thought that was one of the goals."

"It is. But not yet." Even setting an easier pace, Gavin bit the inside of his cheek to keep from climaxing. He moved his hands to Cynthia's back and pulled her forward as he glided up to her shoulder blades.

Her breasts pressed into his chest. An alluring flush decorated her face.

"Can you take more?" he asked.

Aaron squirted a dollop of lube into the palm of his hand.

"More what?" Her question faded into a squeal when Aaron slipped his fingers between her ass cheeks. "Oh." Her lips formed an *O*. "And yes."

Gavin liked the sound of her agreeing.

Aaron fisted his cock, and knelt behind Cynthia. Gavin felt the change in resistance when Aaron entered her. He proceeded slowly, pausing regularly to give Cynthia a chance to adjust.

Gavin enjoyed the torturous, prolonged moment. When Aaron was completely inside Cynthia, Gavin raised his head to draw one of her nipples into his mouth. He licked and sucked, matching Aaron's thrusting speed, and falling into Cynthia's moans.

Her sighs grew to sharp, rapid gasps. She dug her nails into Gavin's arms. Though her eyes were open, she stared at something past him. When she came, she clenched around his shaft, milking him.

The ache of her nails digging into his biceps mingled with the rub of Aaron the slickness of her tunnel. Gavin couldn't hold back. He pounded hard and fast, losing himself in waves of pleasure. Climax spilled through and out of him. A sparkle of lights danced behind his lids, and he grew light-headed.

He recognized Aaron's grunts and knew he was coming too.

It took a few moments, before the chorus of cries, groans, and whimpers faded, leaving gasps for breath in their place.

Aaron slid out of Cynthia, and Gavin helped her roll to the side. She rested her head on his shoulder with a giggle-sigh. Aaron took the spot behind her on the mattress, and draped an arm over her waist. "Disappointed?" he asked, tone light and breathless.

"So far from the opposite, it might as well be another country," she said.

Gavin brushed her hair from her face. It wasn't often he was at a loss for words, but right now, nothing felt adequate. Had it ever been like this when he and Aaron picked someone up?
He shook the question aside before found purchase. Cynthia was fun, unique even, but not worth going all swoony over, even in the throes of post-coital bliss.

*

Aaron glanced at Gavin's sleeping form, and a pleasant thrum pulsed inside. He grabbed his suit coat from where he'd draped it over the back of a chair, gave his partner one last look, and left the bedroom. Gavin hadn't slept through Aaron's getting up in months.

Then again, Aaron hadn't slept so well in ages, either. Last night with Cyn wasn't just great sex; it was also some sort of mental outlet. Between failed investments at work, the resurgence of Gavin's name in the media, and the arguments both caused, the weight on Aaron—on them both—had built to unbearable. It was as though the balloon burst yesterday, but in a good way.

Aaron was right to add the condition to his pending contract with Cyn. Not that he expected this result or could have guessed it, but he was happy with it. There was a whisper of disappointment when all of them agreed it was best she head home at the end of the night, but it passed in a cloud of rationale.

He grabbed his wallet and keys from their post near the front door, and headed out. A light, nameless tune danced through his head as he took the elevator to the main floor of the condo building.

A small pack of people huddled around the security desk. Habit dictated Aaron duck his head and skirt the crowd without making eye contact. As he stepped outside, he realized how silly the habit was. Gavin hadn't had fans stalking him at home in years.

Sun streamed between buildings as it rose, and when Aaron stepped outside, it warmed his face and drew more of his calm to the surface. Might as well walk to the office and enjoy his morning. Some people thought L.A. was all smog and misery, but he loved it here—the sun, the lack of a real winter, and being so close to the ocean despite living in a concrete village.

Twenty minutes later, he stepped into the lobby coffee shop of the building he worked in. The queue snaked toward the door. Fine with him. He wasn't in a hurry. He took his spot and pulled out his phone to browse headlines while he waited.

He stuck to celebrity news. Who was dating, engaged to, or cheating on whom was easier to stomach at an early hour than global politics. He'd catch up on those later in the day.

Former Child Actor Gavin Jackson Doxed

Fuck. Aaron tightened his grip on his phone, concern and fury souring in his gut. Coffee didn't sound appealing anymore. Pictures getting out wasn't a huge deal. Rumors of a career revival were easy to brush off. Having their dinner plans leaked and being interrupted? That sucked a bit.

But home was sacred. It was their safe haven.

Aaron headed for the elevator. His fingers itched to be doing something. He wanted to dial their lawyer now, but this was a conversation best held in the privacy of his office.

As he waited the excruciating seconds for the car to climb to his floor, he followed the links in the article. All sources mentioned Gavin's information was out there, but no one listed the actual address. That was something to be grateful for, wasn't it?

He reached the agency suite, and cut a straight line for his desk.

"Murdock." The receptionist's call stopped him before he was halfway down the hall.

"Yes?"

"VitaStat has called three times. They need an answer today."

Because their fuckup was his priority? Aaron kept the irritated thought to himself. No reason to take it out on her. "Thanks. If they call again in the next half hour, tell them to"—*go fuck themselves*—"sit tight. I'll be with them soon."

"Will do." Her voice faded behind him as he stepped into his office and closed the door. He was settling in front of his computer, when his phone chimed.

The email was from Don. *Saw the news. We're on it.*

The note didn't reassure Aaron the way he wanted. *Keep me posted. Just me,* he replied. Gavin wouldn't take this well, and there was no reason to wake him up just to ruin his day.

Aaron dove into work as much as he could, with the celebrity news lingering at the forefront of his mind. He looked over the VitaStat account again. He didn't like either of his options—extend them more capital that only had a fifty-percent or so chance of putting them back on track, or admit now they weren't going to recover, and eat most of his investment.

A couple updates came in from Don. All of the notices had come down. Like the other day, with the pictures of them coming out of Cyn's office, they couldn't trace the rumors back to a source. But they also didn't find any trace of Aaron and Gavin's home address online.

Aaron had been studying the VitaStat proposal for a few hours, when Gavin called.

"So, it's always great to wake up to my name in the news." Gavin sounded nonchalant.

Aaron swallowed a growl. He'd stressed all morning over that, but this wasn't the time or person to take his frustration out. "It's under control."

"You couldn't drop me a note to let me know that?"

"I've been busy, and I didn't want to get you up before you were ready." A new wave of concern surged inside. Was the crowd in the condo lobby this morning there because of Gavin? Aaron's office line rang, Cyn's number flashing on the screen. He sent it straight to voicemail.

"Because waking up to headlines like that is so much better than hearing it from you?" Gavin chuckled. "I'm serious. It's not a big deal. Not until they start banging on the front door."

A fraction of the weight pressing in on Aaron lifted. "Thank God. You're taking this really well."

"Maybe it's not such a big deal, you know? I'm a big boy, I can deal with a little bad news."

Aaron sighed, pushing out a breath of tension in the process. "Glad to hear it."

"I'll let you get back to work, handsome. See you tonight."

Aaron was feeling better as he disconnected. That went better than he could have possibly imagined. He turned back to his VitaStat numbers. If he set up the new contract correctly, to extend them additional funds, he could give them what they wanted and mitigate his risk. They had a fantastic product—he wouldn't have backed them otherwise. They didn't know much about the business side of things, though. Aaron would install someone in their organization who did.

He worked through lunch, ensuring his math was solid. Cyn called again, and he sent her to voicemail a second time. He'd deal with one decision at a time. Not that he had much to figure out in her case. He was pretty certain her app was a done deal.

A little while later, he dialed VitaStat's founder.

"Hey, man. Glad you didn't forget about us," Shawn greeted him.

Aaron gave a tight laugh. "Not an option. Is now a good time?"

"Depends on what you have to say."

"I'm giving you more money." Might as well cut to the punchline.

"Fantastic." The irritation vanished from Shawn's voice.

Aaron gritted his teeth. "With conditions."

"Sure. Anything."

"I'm installing a new CEO."

"Fuck that." Shawn's tone shifted in a blink. "I'm the CEO."

Aaron gave the phone a thin-lipped smile. Now that he'd made the decision, he'd plow through to the results he needed. "No. You're a board member. You're the head of development. You require a counterpart."

"This is bullshit. You can't oust me. No."

Aaron shrugged. "Funding hinges on it. Let me know your decision in the next twenty-four hours."

Shawn disconnected without a reply.

That went about as well as Aaron expected. He didn't want Shawn to call his bluff; having VitaStat turn down this requirement meant Aaron had to back out now, and that would be costly. But if they couldn't agree to this, they wouldn't survive long enough to be worth an additional investment.

Time for a far more pleasant conversation. He called Cyn.

"I was starting to think you were avoiding me," she answered.

A sliver of doubt gnawed at him, carried on the question, was *last night a mistake?* He shoved it aside. Last night was incredible, and he wasn't letting a couple of bad moments today spoil that. Besides, that was pleasure, this was business. Everyone agreed. "And why would I do that?"

CHAPTER ELEVEN

Cynthia told herself not to fall off a cliff of paranoia. Aaron hadn't called her back because she wasn't his only priority. That was fine. She could wait.

Except her legal issues loomed, and her worry was enhanced by doubts about what happened with Gavin and Aaron—not the sex itself, or even the time leading up to it. But could that line between professional and personal stay sharp and distinct?

Ridiculous. She'd never had an issue with it before. Not that she'd ever slept with a business associate before.

When Aaron returned her call, relief spilled inside, followed by the reminder she was being ridiculous. Of course he'd get back to her. "I was starting to think you were avoiding me." She kept her voice light and teasing.

"And why would I do that?" He sounded pleasant.

That was a good sign. "No reason. The mind plays tricks; that's all. Is now a good time?"

"I called, didn't I?" A tired thread bled into his voice. "What's up?"

She pushed friendly-but-professional to the surface. "I'd like to get on your calendar to discuss next steps on funding my project. See if you're interested in proceeding. Talk about any other requirements. Pencil in how we'd like to move forward. Sooner rather than later, if we can."

"I'll have to check my schedule. This is something we should set aside a decent block of time for."

"You put off a girl too long, and she may start to feel used." She regretted the teasing the moment it was out. She gave a tiny laugh to take the edge off. *Like that's going to help.*

His chuckle wasn't so playful. "How do you think I feel, as the guy holding the wallet?"

"It was a joke." If she glued her smile in place, it would show over the phone line. That was how it worked, wasn't it?

"It was a shitty one. Any specific reason you're pursuing this so hard?"

I don't want to lose my business to my ex-best friend, because I couldn't keep my mouth shut last time I spoke to her. "You know how it goes. I've been waiting a long time to move forward, and now that a solution is in sight, I'm anxious. I don't want to be pushy, though. I can wait."

"Bullshit." He spat out the word with a harsh *crack.*

Her mask slipped, and she clenched her jaw. She had no idea how this conversation went downhill so fast. "Excuse me?"

"I'm sorry." Some of the aggravation faded from his words. "It's a reasonable expectation. But you're hiding something. What aren't you telling me?"

How the hell did he know that? She didn't want to bring up the C&D. Once she dealt with things, it wouldn't be an issue. She fumbled for something else to say, though. Damn it. Why didn't she think this through sooner? Because she hadn't expected him to be so perceptive. Or maybe he was bluffing.

"Cynthia." His tone was sharp. "You don't walk into a business relationship keeping secrets. If this impacts the bottom line, disclose it."

"I didn't develop the app alone." She measured her words, fumbling for the best way to paint the situation.

"Don't make me call this off."

Panic surged inside. "*No*. There's no reason for that. It's not anything that affects you."

"I need to be the judge of that. If it touches your business at all, and it involves money, it involves me."

She had to come clean. She couldn't think of any other way around it. "My roommate developed a lot of the back end code. A while back we had a falling out, and now she wants me to buy her out of her intellectual property." There. That kept any mention of legal issues out of things but was still the truth.

"You didn't think it was important to bring this up sooner? That's the kind of thing you should mention up front." The emotion was fading from his voice, leaving a cool tone in its place.

"I didn't know until a few days ago."

"That you were using her IP?"

"That she was going to sue me for it." Cynthia bit the inside of her cheek. Not what she wanted to say. Despair built inside. Was there any way to salvage things at this point? Sure there was. She'd tell Aaron her plan to buy out Emily, show him it was a viable decision, and beg forgiveness for not mentioning it sooner. He'd had her jump through enough hoops so far, he had to still be interested in the company.

"Fuck. There are lawyers involved?" He didn't seem to be in an understanding mood.

Desperation bled into panic. "Yes. But if I could talk to her, there wouldn't have to be. I could make things better, but I don't know how to get a hold of her." She wasn't helping her situation any.

"You're not on speaking terms. She's suing you. But everything's under control?" It sounded so bad when he put it like that.

"Right now it's a *cease and desist*. No lawsuit yet."

"*Yet*. I'm not forming a partnership with someone accused of IP theft. I don't care if you have the most amazing product in the history of the universe—which you don't—that's a death knell for an investor."

"But there's a buy-out amount. Once that's settled, this goes away. No more issues." Why hadn't she told him about this when she found out? Because she didn't think it was a big deal.

"Did you have a lawyer confirm that?" he asked.

"I can't exactly afford—"

"God damn it, Cynthia. Are you serious?"

She was scrambling for the right thing to say, but nothing came to mind. "If I know I'm being funded, I can make arrangements."

His sigh rattled her thoughts. "Send over a copy of the paperwork, and I'll run it by my attorney. I'm not making any promises, though. I can't walk into a situation like this if there's even the slightest chance it's going to fall apart. Anyone reputable will say the same thing. Hell, *you* should be saying it."

"I'll send it over right now. Thank you."

"Yeah. I'll be in touch, one way or another." The line went dead.

Cynthia set the receiver back in its cradle and tried to swallow the fear crawling through her. Had she lost her only opportunity to make this happen? Washed years of work down the drain? Was two in the afternoon too early for a drink?

*

Gavin tugged on a baseball cap and grabbed his sunglasses. Aaron called it his Superman disguise. Because Clark Kent still looked like Superman, even with the glasses. Gavin's argument was that he'd dyed his hair and wore colored contacts, and most people had no idea who he was. The rest of it only helped add anonymity.

His brain had been reset since last night. The headlines should have freaked him out, but the standard concern wasn't there. He wasn't interested in dealing with fans or the paparazzi, though.

"*Gavin.*" A woman called his name as he

neared Aaron's building.

He gritted his teeth, pulled his hat down lower, and kept walking.

"Gavin Jackson." She stepped in his path with two friends. Her cheeks were flushed dark pink, and a grin threatened to split her face. "It is you, isn't it?"

Years of interacting with fans had him hardwired to not be rude, regardless of how he felt about the interruption. He returned her smile. "That's me." He leaned in and dropped his voice to a stage whisper. "But don't tell. I'm incognito."

A giggle rippled through the small group. "Of course not." She held up her phone and tugged him toward them at the same time. "Can we get a picture with you?"

"Sure." He draped his arms over their shoulders, and let them press their cheeks to his. The interaction wasn't bad—they were all friendly—but the attention they drew made him twitch. Especially when they begged him to take off the hat and sunglasses *or else our friends will never believe it was you.*

He lingered on the hint of smugness that he was right about his Superman disguise.

It felt like an eternity later but was only a couple of minutes, when they thanked him, gave him a hug each, and were on their way.

Gavin couldn't escape the curious stares from passersby fast enough. He ducked into the building Aaron worked in, and moments later, he reached his destination.

Aaron looked up from his computer, tired

lines marring his eyes and forehead. Guilt wormed through Gavin that he'd grumbled over something as simple as a couple of photos when his partner looked like he was having the day from hell.

"You all right?" He crossed the room and kissed Aaron before dropping into an empty chair.

"Long day."

"Sounds like a good excuse to take off a little early, so we can go somewhere and unwind you."

Aaron shook his head. "I can't. I have to run VitaStat paperwork and something for Cyn by Legal, and then get back to this stack of work calling my name."

"If you're at the Legal point with Cynthia, that's a good thing, right?" Gavin asked.

"It's really not."

"What's going on?" Gavin's concern grew.

Aaron's phone rang. "It's Liz. I should take it."

Gavin liked Aaron's business partners. They were intelligent, friendly, and all of them together made a great firm. "I want to say *hello*." Gavin reached over the desk and hit the *Speaker* button. "Hey, Liz. Is this a top-secret kind of phone call?"

"Hey, yourself." She sounded cheerful. "And no, it's not. I just need to finalize whether Aaron will be out here for the vendor summit next month."

Some of the lines faded from Aaron's face. "We're looking forward to it."

"Fantastic. While I have you on the line, how's the Cinderella thing going?" Liz asked.

Aaron sank lower in his seat and pinched the bridge of his nose. "Not good. The founder neglected to disclose that her former business partner is suing her over intellectual property.”

“What?” Gavin was stunned. That didn’t sound like Cynthia. Not that he knew her that well, but she didn’t give a stealing-someone-else’s-idea kind of vibe.

“That sucks.” Liz was sympathetic. “Who’s her business partner?”

Aaron glanced at his monitor. “Emily Lowry.”

“I know her. Well, not personally. It’s more like a three-degrees-of-separation thing,” Liz said.

That was curious.

The way Aaron stared at the phone, it looked like he felt the same way. “How?”

“Everyone with big money in tech knows everyone else.” Liz said it as if it was the most obvious thing ever.

Gavin didn’t agree. “We’re big money in tech, and we don’t know her.”

“I don’t even think she comes from money,” Aaron added. “She was Cynthia’s roommate.”

Liz made a *tsk* sound. “You know me, and I know people who know Ms. Lowry, so it’s the same thing.”

Aaron scrubbed his face. “Not that it matters. I told Cynthia I couldn’t work with her if she was having these kinds of problems up front.”

“You have to.” The insistence came out with more force than Gavin intended. He reined in his response when Aaron raised his brows. “That is—her idea is good. It’s golden.” That wasn’t an exaggeration. Gavin was fascinated by her concept.

"It is a pretty decent proposal." Liz agreed. "I'd hate to see you pass it up over something like this."

Aaron scowled. "*You* passed it up."

"I have too much on my plate, to give her the attention she deserves."

Gavin wouldn't mind giving Cynthia a little more attention, but that wasn't what Liz meant.

"Unless you've got a magic wand of some sort for this situation, I don't think I have a choice but to drop her." Frustration bled from Aaron's words. "She doesn't know how to get a hold of this Emily, she can't even afford legal counsel to deal with the complaint, and I can't invest in a company the owner doesn't have the rights to."

"I can get you contact information," Liz said.

"I— What?" Aaron looked as shocked as he sounded.

Gavin felt his good mood from earlier returning. "Are you sure?"

"Positive." Liz was chipper. "I'll email it over when I've got it. If anyone asks, it came from Andrew."

"Who's Andrew?" Gavin wanted to know.

"Does it matter?"

Aaron twisted his mouth. "I kind of feel like it does."

"Trust me, it doesn't." Liz assured him. "I just hope they can work this out. I'd like to see you with this dating-app thing on your long-term list."

Gavin would, too. "Thank you, Liz. Brilliant as always."

"Yeah, I am. Enjoy your afternoon,

gentlemen." Liz disconnected.

Gavin looked at Aaron. "Is your afternoon getting any better?"

"Don't know yet." Aaron let out a long sigh. "But I'm thinking so."

CHAPTER TWELVE

Cynthia stared at the phone number in Aaron's email. He insisted it belonged to Emily. Cynthia wanted to call, but doubt and more than six months of no communication had her paralyzed. She missed Emily dearly, and at the same time didn't want her to think the dating app was the only reason Cynthia was reaching out.

She was also curious as hell about why it was an international number. Maybe Emily was finally living her dream of traveling.

Cynthia sucked up her courage and dialed. Each new ring in her ear made her wince. *She's not going to pick up.*

The line clicked. "This is Emily."

Cynthia's voice caught, and she forced her hesitation aside. "Hey. It's Cynthia." She braced herself for the line to go dead.

"You got a new number." Emily didn't sound upset or disappointed. In fact, her tone was flat. Impossible to read.

"I'm leasing office space. This is my official work line. And so did you. I hope that means you're seeing the world." The apology Cynthia should be spitting out wouldn't come.

"I didn't expect to hear from you."

This was Cynthia's opening. "I've been looking for you for a while. To say I'm sorry. To grovel until you believe me. You don't have to forgive me, but I'm hoping we can get to a point where you do."

"How'd you get my number?"

"Andrew?" Cynthia read from Aaron's note. "Before you ask, I don't know who that is."

Emily's sigh echoed over the line. "I do."

Cynthia waited for more of an explanation. She wanted to ask if it had anything to do with where in the world Emily was, but they weren't at the point where that kind of familiarity was appropriate. When Emily didn't continue, Cynthia filled in the dead air. "I'm sorry. So completely. About everything I said last time we talked. I was wrong about all of it, and you didn't deserve that, and I don't know how to make it up to you."

"How's Paul?" An edge crept into Emily's voice.

Cynthia swallowed the bile rising in her throat. This wasn't going well. "Homeless and jobless in Texas, last I heard. That was shortly after you moved out."

"What happened?"

"Not a clue beyond that he met a woman online and moved. He's not speaking to me. When I found out it was him who broke your trust and he confirmed it, I kicked him out. He was furious that I took your side. I should have done it a lot sooner."

"Yeah. You should have." Despite the words,

Emily's tone softened.

"I really am sorry."

"I'm kind of over it. I'm still a little pissed, but it led to good things."

A whisper of relief fluttered behind Cynthia's ribs. "I'm hoping we reach a point where I find out what those things are."

"We might."

Cynthia wasn't sure what to say next. If she was going to repay Aaron for getting her this information, she'd need to ask about the app and the legal issues, but she was enjoying the tentative peace too much to spoil the mood.

"How's the Glass-Slipper thing going?" Emily asked. "Is that why you're renting an office? Is it taking off?"

"It's a bit stalled." Was Emily baiting her?

"What happened?" Emily's question sounded genuine.

"Are you serious?"

"No. I don't give a shit about your adult life's work." Emily was sarcastic, but not in a cruel way. "Of course I'm serious."

This had to be a setup. "You filed a *cease and desist,* for me to either stop development or buy out your intellectual property."

"I did not— Oh." Emily paused. "God damn it, Justin."

"What?" A male voice echoed in the background.

Cynthia spun the name against the list in her head and found a fast match. "Justin? The guy who—"

"Yes. One and the same," Emily said. "I didn't file any legal paperwork against you. What's the law firm name?"

Cynthia read it off the letterhead, and Emily's groan cut her off.

"I may have—maybe once—mentioned in passing to Justin that I threatened you, when we were fighting," Emily explained. "But I didn't expect anyone to take that information and run with it." Her voice grew in volume but was muffled, as if she'd pulled the receiver from her mouth to talk to someone else.

"You don't toss around terms like *lawsuit* and *intellectual property theft* and not mean it," Justin shouted loud enough for Cynthia to make out his response.

"What I don't understand is how he knew you were working on it." Emily was speaking into the receiver again, but her voice was still raised.

"I've been pounding the pavement pretty hard for investors," Cynthia said. "I'm guessing half of L.A. knows."

"She's buying our data." That was Justin again. He sounded closer this time.

"It's not— You know what? I'll talk to you when I'm done on the phone." Emily's tone was playful.

Cynthia couldn't help but smile at the interaction. "You sound happy."

"I am. You and I have a lot to catch up on."

"I didn't call because of the money. I don't want you to think that. You deserve your share, but I miss you. I fucked up."

"You did." Emily sighed "But I miss you too. I'll tell Justin to call off the legal dogs."

Cynthia felt the brightest glimmer of hope that she had in a long time. "I'll set you up with a salary or a board position, or whatever I can, as soon as it's an option."

"I'm not worried about it." Emily sounded like she meant it. "And I want to catch up, but it's late here. Call me this weekend, and we'll chat?"

"I will." Cynthia hung up the phone, giddiness dancing inside.

Now she had to convince Aaron to move forward with the next steps. She only needed her luck to hold out a little longer.

* * * *

The fifty Gavin slipped the maître d' was a painless way to guarantee a seat in a quiet back corner of the restaurant. Gavin refused to think too hard about the instinct that compelled him to rest a hand at the small of Cynthia's back and guide her toward their table.

Aaron pulled out a chair for her and pushed it in as she sat.

When she'd met them outside, he thought the way her dress hugged her body was tantalizing. Now the black skirt slid a few inches higher up her thighs, exposing more of her legs. He forced his gaze away and took his seat as Aaron did the same.

Gavin was happy this business deal was happening. Aaron pointed out there were still several weeks of paperwork and due diligence, but it was easy to convince him this was cause to celebrate. Cynthia took a little more work to talk into dinner, to seal the start of their partnership.

As they picked up their menus, Gavin's gaze fell on three women a few tables over. He swore they all turned away with a giggle when he looked in their direction. He shook the observation aside. Habit and experience had him on edge, especially after the rash of articles and the fans in front of Aaron's office the other day, but he couldn't start seeing shadows everywhere. He needed to stow the paranoia. Until recently, people recognizing him was a rare thing.

The waiter took their orders. For a second, Gavin considered ordering a glass of wine. He opted for the seltzer with a slice of lemon instead.

"I've been wondering…" Cynthia said. "I'm not sure I should ask, but curiosity is winning out."

Gavin braced himself for a question about his career. Or the end of it.

Instead, Cynthia looked at Aaron. "Make me understand the deal with the Picasso. You explained it, but I don't think I understand."

Gavin let out a chuckle of relief. He didn't have to ask, to know what the Picasso reference meant, but he was surprised she had any information about a scam like that. Aaron wasn't usually open about his past.

Cynthia pursed her lips and looked at him. "I'm not dim. I *get it*, but not."

"What bit has you confused?" Aaron asked.

"I can't place my finger on exactly what feels off. If I understand it right, the game works like this. Someone claims to own a piece of art they can't identify. A relative left it to them, or it found its way into their possession in a similar manner. Then they describe a piece a collector knows is rumored lost but incredibly valuable."

Aaron nodded. "Sounds right so far."

Cynthia furrowed her brow. "If no one nibbles at the bait, she has a partner in the crowd who knows to raise the stakes. He offers her a pittance of money, or ups the bid if someone else doesn't offer as much as they want."

"Right again." Gavin swore he could see the gears in her head turning and reflected in her contemplative expression.

"And your conman—woman, whatever—is banking that at least one person in the crowd will decipher what piece she's describing, but won't be honest enough to tell her the truth. Instead, they *take pity* on the poor woman who got gypped out of her inheritance. They offer her pocket change, in comparison to what the real art is worth. A few thousand dollars, to take the worthless piece of art off her hands. That's how they phrase it to her, anyway. But the buyer believes it's actually worth hundreds of thousands, if not millions, and intends to keep it for themselves for pennies on the dollar."

Gavin ginned. "Sounds like you understand it fine."

"That means the scam only works on someone who's willing to be as dishonest as the person running the game." Cynthia sounded curious, rather than bothered.

Aaron looked somber. It made sense. He had firsthand knowledge of how this worked and didn't like delving into that part of his past. "Yup."

"I guess that makes it a little hard to get upset about, but…" Cynthia trailed off.

Aaron raised his brows. "Hmm?"

"What if the seller is telling the truth, and they do have that one rare piece and don't know it? You seem convinced it's always a con."

"It always is." There was no hesitation in Aaron's voice. "But if it was that once-in-a-lifetime find, there would be other signs. Seeing that takes a bit of instinct."

The food arrived, and Gavin nibbled at his dish while he watched the conversation unfold. This had to be difficult for Aaron to delve into, but he didn't look fazed. Something sharp and unpleasant sparked inside Gavin. Jealousy? That didn't make sense. About what? He'd known this story for more than a decade. It wasn't as though he wasn't privy to Aaron's past. And it wasn't guilt over what *they* had done; he and Aaron operated within legal limits with their IPO.

"And you know all of this because— You didn't get taken, did you?" Concern leaked into Cynthia's voice.

Gavin marveled at the contrast of innocence and cynicism in her line of thought.

"The opposite." Aaron corrected her. "I used to do the taking."

"What?" Cynthia looked perplexed.

"Not me, specifically." Aaron's dinner sat untouched. "When I was little, my dad…" He sighed. "A woman like the one at the gallery relies on sex appeal and seeming helpless to draw in her crowds.

My father didn't have the tits or poise to pull that off. Instead, he was the starving father who just needed a few bucks to feed his kid, and he had a rare coin. In his version of the con, a friend told him the coin was worth a couple hundred dollars. His mark would think it was worth thousands but would tell him otherwise. It usually sounded something like, *I'm sorry, man; the coin is worthless. But I can't watch a kid go hungry. I'll give you a hundred bucks for it.*

"And no one ever told him they thought the money was worth more?" Cynthia asked in disbelief.

Aaron shook his head. "Never. Not once. But so you don't think the entire world is made up of shitty people, part of the scam is reading the mark. Dad never approached anyone he thought would either catch him or be honest with him."

"Wow." Cynthia stabbed one vegetable after another, until her fork was a mini-skewer, but she didn't eat. "It must have sucked for you to grow up with that. I'm sorry."

Gavin felt a swell of ambivalence at her response. It was too perfect. "Really."

"Yes, really. I'm not heartless. That sounds miserable." Cynthia was indignant.

"It's not that he doubts your sincerity." Aaron let out a light laugh. "Most people's first response is assuming the apple doesn't fall far from the tree, and that I must be the same way."

"You run a long, tedious game if that's the case. But I would have been the person to either tell your dad the coin was worthless or offer him its true value."

"And Dad wouldn't have seen you as a

mark.”

"Excuse me,” a timid, female voice interrupted the conversation. "Can we get a picture with you?”

An invisible fist clenched around Gavin's chest. It was the women from the other table, who he tried to pretend weren't pointing and whispering. Just as quickly, he spilled numbness through his veins and grinned. "Evening ladies.”

"We're eating." The good cheer vanished from Aaron's voice.

That wouldn't do. Couldn't be rude to the fans. Gavin hated that the instinct to please existed, but he'd never been able to shake it. He looked at Cynthia. "It'll only take a minute, if you're okay with it." It was a manipulative thing to do. He knew she'd be polite, and if she agreed, Aaron wouldn't make a scene.

"It's fine." Cynthia's smile was thin.

Gavin slid into the skin of *friendly celebrity* without further thought, smiling and signing napkins. Except once the first group approached, another couple of women did, and then a husband and wife.

The lines in Aaron's forehead deepened with each new handshake and flash. Gavin regretted having talked himself into this position. He should have let Aaron shoo the first people off, forty-five minutes ago. *Can't be mean to the fans*. The old, familiar voice nagged at Gavin. *Never let them see you at anything but your best*. He was making a bet with himself about how long until Aaron snapped, when a restaurant employee approached.

"Excuse me." The man didn't sound

apologetic in the least. "You're disrupting the other customers. I have to ask you to leave."

"Of course. We were just going." Aaron tossed a large bill on the table, and stood. "I'm sorry, ladies and gents," he said to the small group of people gathered around. "Mr. Jackson needs to be on his way."

A chorus of groans and protests rose up, but Aaron acted as a barrier and led Gavin and Cynthia out through a back door. Once they were outside, people and hot humid air brushing past them without a second glance, Gavin's head started to clear.

"What was that?" Aaron asked in a low voice.

Gavin shrugged and tried to look sheepish. "I didn't want to be rude." It sounded weak, even to him, despite it being as close to the truth as anything. He turned to Cynthia, rather than face Aaron's glare. "Are you free a bit longer? We'll go dancing. Someplace dark, where we won't be interrupted." *And where it's too loud to talk.*

Cynthia bit her bottom lip and looked between him and Aaron, as if she didn't want to take sides.

Gavin leaned in and whispered, "I promise it's fine."

"I'm in if you both are."

She thought she was being magnanimous, but her answer was as good as a *yes.* Aaron wouldn't argue if she was interested.

A twinge of guilt swelled inside Gavin at the manipulation, but he stowed it. He got what he wanted. No need to ruin a perfectly good setup.

CHAPTER THIRTEEN

Cynthia hadn't been dancing in ages. The reminder made her miss Emily. She had no doubt this would be an experience of a whole new sort. And it sounded like fun.

She didn't like the tension that flowed between Gavin and Aaron since the first group of women interrupted dinner, but they insisted they were fine with another stop.

"It'll be fun." Gavin traced his fingers down her arm, raising goosebumps, and grasped her fingers. He tugged playfully. "We'll keep our hands to ourselves, unless you beg."

She tried to give him an incredulous look, but her smile broke through. It did sound tempting. It also sounded like something other than celebrating a business decision with associates. Then again, both men were capable of keeping the physical separate from the emotional, as was she, so they could avoid messy complications if things went further than dancing. "When you put it that way… All right."

Some of the lines of tension faded from Aaron's expression. Cynthia thought it was an odd thing to relax over, but she was grateful to see it. She didn't want to be a catalyst for them arguing.

Aaron pointed them in a different direction. "There's a club within walking distance."

"That's convenient." She teased. "A girl might feel set up."

"Maybe. Maybe not." Gavin's tone was light. "Makes you wonder, doesn't it?"

Aaron shook his head. "Don't listen to him. We like the club. We like the restaurant. Your company is the cherry on top."

She could get used to this kind of attention. Which was a bad idea. After tonight, she was going back to business as usual. There was no harm in everyone enjoying themselves, as long as she didn't let herself believe it was more than *just fun*.

The night air was humid and warm, kissing her arms and legs, and when they reached the club ten minutes later, she was grateful to step into the air conditioning.

Two things struck her first—it was loud, and it was dark. As her eyes adjusted, she saw how many people packed the dance floor. They must have the air set on *frigid*, to keep temps so cool in here.

She and Emily never hit up a place this high end. This wasn't college kids in jeans and T-shirts, grinding against each other because they were stressed from school and desperate to get laid. The place was full of men and women in suits and ties and dresses. Grinding against each other because they were stressed from work and desperate to get laid.

Gavin settled his hands on her hips and pressed his chest to her back. He was firm and steady.

A pleasant shiver ran down her spine. "What do you think?" he asked, his mouth close enough to her ear she heard him without him yelling.

Aaron stood in front of her, attentive gaze saying as much as words could.

She glanced back at Gavin. "It's perfect."

He nudged her toward Aaron, who pulled her onto the dance floor. The heat of gyrating bodies was a sharp contrast to the chill in the air, and the patches flowed over her nerves, heightening her senses. With Gavin and Aaron on either side of her, it was easy to lose herself in the beat.

The scents of sweat and alcohol mingled with a wash of perfumes and deodorants, singeing her sinuses and lingering on her tongue. The flash of neon from above the bar was the only real source of light in the room. The experience was a non-stop assault on the senses. It would be jarring most of the time, but tonight she liked diving into it head first.

Gavin glided his hands up her sides, brushed her breasts, then moved back down to grip her hips. Aaron slid his body against hers, his torso hard and unyielding against her chest. It was intoxicating.

When she stepped aside though, the two of them together at least as good—Gavin dropping down the length of Aaron's body, and gliding up gracefully; the way their lips met before they drifted apart; the spark of passion that flowed between them, almost visible in the dim club.

It was too intimate to watch, but Cynthia couldn't pull her gaze away. It was sobering to see the two locked in a world of their own, in the middle of this chaos—a sharp reminder she was the one-night stand.

It was also intensely erotic. She could feel the desire flowing from them as Aaron scraped his teeth along Gavin's neck, before stealing another kiss. Dampness and arousal grew between Cynthia's thighs. She was tempted to find a corner and finger herself to the images of Gavin and Aaron dancing, seared in her mind. It was dark enough she could probably get away with it.

She was lost in the fantasy, and started when Aaron gripped her waist and pulled her back between them.

"We don't want to leave you out." His breath was hot against her neck.

She shook her head. "That's not how I felt." She had to shout to be heard. Did anyone else hear that? Did she care? *No.* "I was enjoying the show."

"Really?" Gavin moved into her space. He trailed his fingers down her spine, while Aaron splayed his palm on her stomach. "Tucking away memories for later?"

"Yes." She should be embarrassed or something, to admit that aloud, but it was too easy to let go with these two. "For next time I'm alone." She kept her pout playful.

"You shouldn't wait that long." Aaron's mouth vibrated against her skin.

"I can't exactly feel myself up here." It was tempting. No one was paying attention. No one would see. Then again, with the charged atmosphere in the room, if someone *did* see, they probably wouldn't mind. The idea tightened in her nipples, making them strain against her dress.

Gavin leaned in, inches from Aaron. "I'd watch, if you did," he said. "And I promise not to tell." He moved to her side, his body blocking his actions from anyone else's view, lifted up her skirt, and hooked his thumb in the waist of her panties. He shimmied down her frame as he dragged the underwear to the floor.

She stepped out, and he tucked the lingerie in her purse. Cold air kissed her wet mound, the sudden exposure making her slick and coating the inside of her thighs.

"I'm not doing anything in the middle of the dance floor." She tried to keep the quaver from her voice.

"Don't be ridiculous." Aaron said. "The angle out here is all wrong." He grabbed her fingers and pulled her toward a booth near the back of the room. He slid onto the bench and tugged her on his lap, facing away from him.

His erection was rock hard beneath her, digging into her ass and teasing. Was he going to fuck her? Here? That wasn't what she should be asking herself, but—God—she liked the idea.

Gavin scooted in next to them, sitting sideways with one knee on the bench. He rested a hand on her leg and dragged his fingers along the inside of her thigh as he inched his way toward her sex.

Aaron kissed along the back of her neck. "Can we have a semi-private show? You don't have to expose yourself. Feeling you squirm against me when you come will be its own reward."

"I'll help." Gavin sought out her hand,

covered it with his, and used both to pull up the middle of her skirt. The table and his position would probably hide them from view, but she still felt a tingle of excitement and just the right amount of filthy at the sensation of him spreading her legs and exposing her bare pussy in a crowded bar.

Aaron slipped one hand inside her dress from behind and sought out her breast. When he pinched her nipple, she whimpered.

Gavin guided her fingers to her clit. "Show me how you like it."

She couldn't argue. Didn't have the desire or the voice. With Aaron kneading her breast and Gavin's touch following hers, she traced circles around her swollen sex. Climax built inside, carried on the notion that this was so wrong and felt so good. Her fingers were slick with her juices, and she rubbed hard, driving right to the edge.

Frustration built inside when she couldn't slide over. Gavin shoved three fingers inside her without warning, stretching her open. He hooked them up and pumped in time to her self-attentions. Orgasm spilled through her, and she bit the inside of her cheek until it ached, to keep from crying out.

She slowed to a stop as the pleasure ebbed. Gavin raised her hand to his mouth and licked it clean, before offering her his. She sucked herself from his fingers, relishing the expression on his face as she took her time moving from one to the next. It was amazing, but it wasn't enough. "We need to go somewhere with fewer… restrictions," she said. She leaned back into Aaron and tilted her head toward his. "I want you inside me."

*

Aaron was grateful for the loose slacks he wore. He was hard enough he might have popped his zipper in jeans. And with Cyn in his lap, digging into him and writhing in pleasure, he almost came. He was tempted to drag her into the nearest bathroom stall, pin her to the wall, and fuck her until she screamed louder than the music.

At the same time, he wanted whatever came next to last longer than five minutes. "Let's get out of here." He helped her stand and smooth out her skirt, unable to contain his smirk when she wobbled.

Knowing there was nothing underneath didn't help his tentative leash on self-control.

The three wove their way toward the exit.

"Excuse me." A woman stepped in Gavin's path. "You're Gavin Jackson? Can I have an autograph?" She produced a Sharpie and tugged down the neck of her dress, exposing most of her breast.

Right. This was why Aaron was in a foul mood earlier. How did he forget? But this was the equivalent of interrupting sex. Gavin would turn her down, and they could be on their way.

"Sure, doll." Gavin took the pen from her and signed her skin.

Aaron's irritation dialed up a notch, and his arousal crept back in response. He forced calm through his veins and grabbed Gavin's hand. "We should be going."

But a pair of men stood in front of them, and

as Aaron looked around the room, he realized several pairs of eyes were on them. "We should be going," he repeated in Gavin's ear, unable to suppress his growl.

"Ten minutes." Gavin waved him off. "Can't be rude."

Of all the bad habits Gavin learned in Hollywood, this was the one Aaron loathed most—the insistence it was wrong to turn away fans. Aaron glanced at Cyn, who stood to the side, lips pursed in a frown.

More of the people watching pressed in, to get closer to Gavin, shoving Aaron and Cyn further back in the process.

Aaron gripped Cyn's hand. "I'm sorry," he mouthed.

Her weak smile vanished into blankness as quickly as it appeared. "I can stick around for five minutes. No worries.

Half an hour later, the crowd around Gavin was bigger. "Hey, handsome." He grinned at a guy who handed him a pen and a cocktail napkin. "Autograph in exchange for a sip of your drink?"

The stranger was happy to comply. So were the next several people Gavin made the same offer to.

Aaron clenched his fist and counted to ten. He hated to be a wet blanket, but Gavin drunk—off the wagon twice in as many months—was a bad thing. He was a sweet enough drunk, but it was the downward slide that tended to follow that made Aaron's gut clench.

He tried to push through the throng of people,

to cut Gavin off.

"I should go." Cyn's voice barely reached him.

He glanced back, not blaming her. He gave her a tight smile and nodded, and she spun away.

"Cynthia," Gavin called over the chatter. "Where are you going?"

Aaron didn't know which bothered him more—the slur in Gavin's question, or that he stopped her when he refused to listen to Aaron's requests to go.

Gavin reached past everyone and grabbed Cynthia's wrist. He pulled her to stand next to him and draped an arm over her shoulder. Her scowl deepened.

"This woman here"—he pointed to Cyn—"is a fucking genius. She's the smartest, sexiest matchmaker in all of L.A."

Cyn's smile was thin. She broke away and shoved through the crowd, ignoring Gavin's calls for her to stop. Aaron followed her outside. Gavin could fend for himself, if he was going to be an asshole.

"Cyn, please." Aaron's voice sounded unnaturally loud to his ringing ears.

She paused. "It's not your fault. Stay with your guy. I'll call a cab."

Fuck. Cockblocked by his own boyfriend. It wasn't the first concern Aaron should have, but it amused him in a twisted sort of way. He was tempted to take Cyn home. Not even to finish what they started, but because she didn't deserve to be brushed aside this way. But as annoyed as he was with Gavin, he couldn't abandon him. Not completely. "I'll wait with you until your ride gets here. I can do that much," Aaron said.

"Where're you going?" Gavin pushed between them. A wash of alcohol rushed over Aaron's face, and he cringed.

"Home." Cyn's voice was flat.

Gavin frowned and stepped back. "You can't. I'll behave." The slur faded from his words, but it didn't vanish. "The fans are gone, and I'll be good. I promise. We'll go back to our place, away from everyone. I didn't mean to spoil the night."

Aaron clenched his jaw until it ached. What the fuck was this?

Cynthia glanced at him, and the creases in her forehead grew more pronounced. "No. I'm done."

Aaron didn't know if he was more grateful or perturbed. Either way, he didn't blame her.

CHAPTER FOURTEEN

Gavin woke up with his head pounding and the spot next to him in bed empty. He rubbed his temples at the assault of images from last night. The deluge of reminders. It had been years since he had a morning like this—where part of him wished blackout drunk was one of the cards in his deck of miserable results of fucking up an evening.

A bottle of water sat on his nightstand. It drew an almost-smile. He downed half of it in a single gulp. God, he fucked up big time. While it was happening, it all seemed harmless. With the fans pressing in, he had to be polite, but that kind of friendliness was different than screen acting. He couldn't become someone else and slide into a role. He had to be himself, but a better, kinder, more-sociable version.

Gavin had seen Aaron's irritation. Cynthia's too. He didn't blame them, but the insistence in his head wouldn't let him break away. *Never let the fans down*. The first drink was to take the edge off. A sip of someone else's booze wasn't the same as drinking, right? By Number Ten or Twelve, he'd stopped caring. The alcohol worked better than he expected.

His head spun with regret, but the room had stopped. Aaron's half of the bed didn't look slept in. *Fuck.* Gavin had some serious groveling to do.

He found Aaron in their office. His computer was on, but he wasn't doing anything.

Gavin lingered in the doorway. Best to approach this contritely. "Thanks for the water."

Aaron started but didn't turn. He grabbed the mouse and clicked, then scrolled through the page too fast to be registering anything. "Mhmm."

"I'm sorry about last night."

"Okay."

Gavin's sour gut twisted in on itself until it was a pretzel. "Please don't be mad?"

Aaron's shoulders rose and fell with his heavy sigh. He finally spun in his chair. "Seriously?"

"If I'm going to make it better, I have to start somewhere."

"You start by not doing it in the first place. Like you promised you wouldn't, two months ago. You know—the last time."

The edge in Aaron's voice caught Gavin off guard. This wasn't the way the conversation went. Not ever. Gavin apologized. Aaron understood and accepted.

Gavin crossed the room and crouched in front of Aaron, to look him in the eye. He took Aaron's hands. "You're right, and I'm sorry. I don't have better words than that; the only thing I can do is prove to you I mean it."

"How?"

"Give me time, and I'll show you." This was a good step. Gavin hid his smile. He could make things right. "Don't give up on me yet. I'll make it up to you. I'll make things right with Cynthia."

Aaron's jaw tightened. "Cynthia's a business associate. She's a lot of fun, but you realize *that* part of the relationship is over, don't you?"

"Of course I do." Gavin's grin was in defiance of the surge of disappointment gnawing at his insides. "I owe her an apology; that's all. But I'm worried about you and me. I want—I need—us to be okay."

Aaron sighed. "We will be. But only if you can put this behind you. If you're going to sign autographs, mingle with the fans—whatever—I don't have a problem with it. But you have to walk away when it pushes your buttons, rather than grabbing the nearest drink."

"I know. You're right." Gavin would say whatever it took at this point. He was so close to getting that reconciliation. Besides, he'd spent years avoiding situations like that. He'd go back to being cautious.

Aaron nodded at his computer. "You need to mean it. Really, truly mean it. Because I don't think we can avoid situations like last night anymore. Someone leaked where we were at dinner and at the club. They had a bead on us all night."

Gavin registered what was on the screen, and he grabbed the mouse to scroll through more. Shots of the three of them at dinner. On the street. Dancing. Some were from a distance—grainy and hard to see. Others were entirely too clear and sharp for Gavin's liking. At least there was none of what happened at the table, with Cynthia. That didn't stop a combination of dread and fury from bubbling inside.

He forced his apologetic but cheerful mask to stay in place. "I'm good. I'm sincere about it. I'll show you."

"All right." Aaron cupped his cheek and turned his face, then brushed a kiss across his lips. "I believe you. We'll get through it together. I'm willing to try as long as you are."

"I promise." A whisper in the back of Gavin's head asked if he meant that, and he balled it up with the news that someone was following them when they went out, lit it with a mental match, and let it burn to ashes.

* * * *

Cynthia had been waiting for this moment for months, pounding the pavement, making the pitch, begging and praying to whatever gods were listening to give her a chance to make this business take off. She only needed a little capital. Enough seed money to get the ball rolling.

Now that she was moving forward, that opportunity hovering in front of her—available as long as the next steps went all right—discomfort chewed at her thoughts. If she didn't have so much riding on this, she'd give into the impulse to not see Aaron or Gavin again.

Everything hinged on it, though. So when Aaron approached her in the investment firm lobby, she smiled, shook his hand, and followed him into his office.

He nodded at the seat across from his desk,

and took his own when she sat.

"How are you?" Cynthia wasn't sure if her question held hidden meaning, or if she was simply being polite.

Aaron's smile was thin. "Great. Glad to be moving forward with this. I hope you're prepared for several hours of intensive paperwork review."

Polite it was. She could do this—pretend the weekend never happened. After all, that was Cyn who hooked up with the guys for a little fun. Cynthia didn't have flings with business associates. "Absolutely. In a twisted way, I'm looking forward to it."

"Fantastic. Let's dive right in. Some of this may seem like a random order, but it helps me keep things straight in my head, so…" He trailed off with a frown.

She waited a few seconds, not wanting to interrupt. When he didn't continue, she prompted. "So…?"

"Right." He shook his head. "Stick with me, and it'll all come together over the next few days and weeks. Some things take more time to process and verify. We cover those first, and then move on to the rest."

"I trust you."

The creases in Aaron's forehead deepened. "Do you?"

"Yes." The answer slipped out without thought, but she didn't see any reason not to. "Are you sure you're okay?"

"Yup. Never better." His words fell flat.

Was this about what happened at the club?

Any of it? Was it about her in general? Was she just being paranoid? Though she was here to discuss business, she needed to clear the air. Maybe she was reading too much into something that wasn't related to her at all, but she was going to be working closely with Aaron over the next several months, and after that he'd be a member of her board, so she might as well get her concerns out of the way now. "Stop me if I'm being presumptuous, but does your mood have anything to do with the other night?"

"Yes. But not the way I suspect you think."

Now she was as curious as she was concerned. "May I pry?"

"I should say *no*"—Aaron raked his fingers through his hair—"but I don't want to brush you off. At the very least, I need to apologize for how the evening ended."

She'd been pissed that night. Gavin's behavior made her uncomfortable on so many levels. He radiated a lack of control she didn't like. Over the next day or two, she reconciled with it. "I appreciate it, but it's done and over. All of it." She might as well reinforce her perspective now. The thought of saying with finality, *it was fun, but it's done*, made her joints ache, but there was no better time. "We all agreed we'd have some fun, it wouldn't interfere with work, and we'd move on after."

"I appreciate that." Aaron's tone implied he didn't, or she was reading too much into it. "I still… Never mind. You don't need to hear about my personal life."

"Are you going to talk to *someone* about it?"

"What?"

"Whatever is going on, it's obviously eating you. Can you tell Gavin?" That was a stupid question. Even if Aaron's grimace didn't make her regret it, asking was crossing a line.

"No."

She recoiled at the force in his reply.

"I didn't mean to snap." Ice slid in, to hide any other tone in Aaron's voice.

She composed herself. "Don't worry about it. It wasn't appropriate for me to ask. If we're all right, we can get to work."

"Great idea." He slid a paperclipped stack of printouts across the desk. "First, we can't go much further without appropriate patents, copyrights, and trademarks on file. For the product and the company. If you have the information already, I need copies of the documents listed here. If not, now's the time to file."

"I think I have all of it, but I'll double check, and get you the final information. How did the two of you meet?" *No. Wrong. Stupid.* She meant to ask if there was anything specific she should pay attention to.

"We were childhood sweethearts. Next step is—"

"No shit. Childhood sweethearts?" Cynthia ducked her head when Aaron scowled. She wasn't sure if his reaction was because of her question or interruption, but either way she shouldn't have done it. "I'm sorry. I'm overstepping so many boundaries."

He scrubbed his face, and when he met her gaze again, some of the lines of tension had faded.

"My boyfriend fingered you in a packed dance club, while I watched. I don't think we have a lot of boundaries anymore."

Heat—both from embarrassment and traces of the memory—scorched her skin. She pushed aside the reaction. "Is this where you tell me your deepest, darkest secrets?" she teased.

"I don't have these kinds of skeletons." His laugh sounded natural. "But I will tell you the story about how Gavin and I met, if you're actually interested."

"I am."

He let out a long breath. "I told you about the scams I used to help my dad run. When I was fourteen, the law caught up to us, and he was arrested. It wasn't the first time, but technology had come far enough that his fake IDs and background didn't hold up under scrutiny. The police traced his identification back to warrants in other states, and he was looking at spending months or years behind bars, instead of a weekend or two."

"I'm sorry. That sounds awful for you." Cynthia had no idea what she expected as an opener in a story of young love that was still alive for Aaron and Gavin at thirty, but this wouldn't have made the list.

Aaron shrugged. "I don't think of it as something bad or good. It just was. I didn't want to go into foster care, so I hid from the system. I'd learned enough from Dad that it was easy to run cons myself. Everyone felt sorry for the poor kid, and on my own, that sympathy was even easier to game. But I wasn't doing anything big time, or even midrange, like he had. My gigs were as much performance art as anything—card tricks, shell games… And movie lots were my best bet. Hollywood loves a show."

"Including Gavin?" As the story unfolded, it filled her with a combination of awe and horror for what Aaron must have gone through.

"Everyone *but* Gavin." Aaron's chuckle was laced with melancholy. "First day we met, I was behind the lot he was shooting in, playing Find the Queen with a battered deck of cards. I had a standard crowd of people who watched. I was pretty sure some were there more out of pity than anything, but whatever kept me fed and off the streets was fine with me. Gavin called me on my bullshit. I loved it. The gorgeous, famous actor talking to me *and* recognizing what I was up to." Aaron faltered. "From there, we became fast friends, and a few years down the line, more."

Cynthia had a feeling he was holding something back, but she'd already pried too much. "It sounds like an incredible journey from then to now."

"It was. It *is*." Sadness tinged his voice.

That almost made her ask for more, but she wasn't going to indulge her curiosity at the risk of opening a can of worms that couldn't be closed. "We should get back to work."

Aaron gave her a grateful smile. "Thanks."

CHAPTER FIFTEEN

Aaron slogged through the next several days, unsure where things stood at home, or even where he wanted them to be. Gavin was a saint, not reacting when Aaron came home in a foul mood or pulled away. Just being there.

Still, Aaron felt like each day in the office was a chance to breathe. Working with Cynthia was a pleasant distraction, and diving into his other investments kept his mind as busy.

He was pondering that, and failing to ignore a fresh wave of guilt, when he walked into the office Friday morning.

"Jonathan is looking for you." The receptionist's statement pulled Aaron out of his head.

He flashed her a smile. "Thanks." He set his stuff next to his desk, strolled down the hall to his business partner's door, and knocked on the frame.

Jonathan looked up, and a whisper of a frown crossed his face before vanishing. "Hey. You have a few minutes?"

"That's why I'm here." Aaron dropped into the seat across from him and crossed one ankle over the other knee. "What's up?"

"You read the news this morning?"

Aaron shook his head. "Avoiding it right now. Makes it easier to start my day."

Jonathan let out a slow hiss. "Lucky me. A couple of the other partners wanted to ambush you with this, but not all of us thought that was the best approach, so consider this your heads-up."

"About…?" Aaron didn't like the dread that clawed inside, threatening his tentative calm. He chose to ignore the handful of alerts about Gavin this morning. None had been critical this week, and Don was on top of things, so Aaron wanted to enjoy the peace for a few hours before he followed up.

"Your name is smeared all over financial news."

"Wait. *My* name?"

Jonathan scrubbed his face. "They're calling you the Four Billion Dollar Fraud. Apparently there's a source that can prove the deal you brokered a few years back—the company you built and sold— none of that was your doing."

I signed the paperwork. Aaron didn't suspect that was the right answer. "I sold a tech startup for four billion dollars. Of course there were other people involved." It was a weak response.

The way Jonathan raised his brows said he agreed. "I'll be more direct. The hype machine that inflated the company's worth, the data, the perfect storm of product features… Was that you?"

"I played the offers off each other." Aaron suspected this wouldn't help his case. Years ago, Gavin found a distraction from his addictions. It was part of what helped in his recovery. He had the notion he could create the perfect tech startup, with the perfect product at its base, from a marketing perspective. Then he just had to spin the hype to make the company worth millions.

He did better than his wildest dreams. Had investors and offers coming in, left and right. Everyone was talking about this great new thing, but the last thing Gavin wanted was to be in the spotlight. So they stuck Aaron's name on everything. "Does it matter who handled what?" It did, for some aspects of the deal, but he hoped otherwise. "Every partner knew the details of the sale when I joined the firm."

"Except that one little piece of information that you didn't think the deal up. None of us is just here because we had the cash to buy in. We each bring different skills to the table, except yours apparently aren't yours."

The words stung, but they were true. This was one of those things Aaron preferred not to think about. "Where does this lead? You said some of the other partners wanted to ambush me."

"This is the kind of tiny little lie that reflects poorly on the firm. If we claim our partners are responsible for—and capable of—things they aren't, it looks bad for all of us. Some of the others want you gone, no questions asked. Not all of us agree. You have an hour to figure out if you can spin this in your favor and make your case to the rest of us. We can't wait any longer. We have to do damage control."

Aaron understood the logic, but he didn't like being on this end of the decision. A bubble of frustration surged inside, and he burst it. This wasn't Jonathan's fault. Aaron brought it on himself.

"Thanks. Main conference room at nine, then?"

"Yup."

Aaron tried to call Gavin but didn't get an answer. Both their names were on this. After all this time, and with everything happening recently, this would bring even more publicity down on them. On Gavin.

And Aaron couldn't focus on that yet. He needed to figure out what to say. If he were fifteen years younger, he'd prepare for a conversation full of misdirection. Turn every question back on the person who asked it and let the other partners talk themselves out of any negative decision.

There was a big problem with heading down that road, besides the fact that it was a huge deception. Once he started something like that, it meant a lifetime of keeping up the act. Constantly being on his guard if someone at the firm took issue with his past. Besides, it made him too much like Gavin—pretending the problem didn't exist.

He regretted the thought the moment he had it. Gavin didn't deserve that.

When Aaron walked into the meeting, an odd cocktail of dread and acceptance filled him. He made the same statement for his case that he'd made with Jonathan. Every partner knew the details of the original deal, the only thing that was different were some of the roles people took in the sale of Aaron's old company.

"The issue is that the role you let us believe was yours is the reason we invited you to join us. It's one of the selling points of this firm." Bernie was one of the partners Aaron had never gotten along with.

There was no open hostility, but Aaron wasn't surprised to see him leading this conversation. "The skills you're supposed to have seem to belong to someone else, as is evidenced in the string of poor investment decisions you've made."

Aaron clenched his jaw. "It's been a few miscalculations, and you know that. I went through due diligence every time—"

"This isn't about looking at numbers on paper," Bernie said. "There's an instinct that's required for working in venture capital, and it's one you seem to be lacking."

"It sounds like you've already made up your mind." Aaron struggled to keep the bitterness from his voice. "If I continue to make my case, will I be heard?"

"If you'd walked into the room with proof this morning's report was false, we would have listened. As far as public record is concerned, this is an amicable parting of ways. You agreed that it was best you pursue your interests separately." Bernie's smirk defied the calm, rehearsed words.

"Any investments you made with other partners or at the firm level, stay with the firm." Liz's voice echoed from the speaker phone. Though Aaron couldn't see her, he suspected her words were kinder than Bernie's. "Any that are yours alone are between you and those individuals. There are a few of those some of us are interested in, if you don't want to pursue those partnerships. We'll get with you individually."

Aaron wanted to protest. He should have gone with the redirection approach. At least then he'd have a little longer to figure out how to keep this from falling apart. There were better uses for his energy, though. Salvaging the business partnerships he still had, for instance. "I understand."

More details were exchanged, but Aaron only half listened. It would all be written up minutes later, and he could review it. Now, he was busy figuring out how to save his stake in the companies that he retained interest in.

He returned to his office, and his heart sank when he saw Gavin hadn't gotten back to him. As much as he needed to focus on the morning's events, his attention would be divided until he knew Gavin was all right. He could do this work from home. He gathered his stuff, told the receptionist where he could be reached, and headed back to the condo.

The house was quiet when he stepped inside. "Gavin? You around?"

No answer. A quick search of the place revealed Aaron was alone. It was a little after noon. Maybe Gavin went to grab lunch. He'd been more or less hiding the past several days. It would be good if he stepped out.

A little odd, if he'd read the news this morning, but maybe he was handling it better than Aaron. It wasn't about Gavin's Hollywood career, so it may have glanced off him.

The idea gnawed at Aaron, and he refused to dive into figuring out why. Instead, he turned back to his work. There was a lot of legal paperwork to sift through, and a lot of business associates to reach out to. He needed to get started.

Aaron managed to pour most of his focus into

work, and the next time he looked up, it was after six. He rubbed his eyes, to restore the moisture to them. Where the hell was Gavin? He tried calling again, and Gavin's ringtone greeted him from the bedroom. Aaron followed the noise to find Gavin's phone sitting on the nightstand.

Which didn't mean anything. It wasn't as though Gavin was out getting wasted. He took off for a few hours and forgot his phone. Big deal.

By eleven that night, Aaron hovered on a knife's edge between concern and fury. If Gavin was out drinking or anything similar, while Aaron was here worrying and fighting to hold his career together—

"Honey, I'm home." Gavin's cheerful call carried through the house.

Aaron stepped into the living room. "Where the fuck were you?"

CHAPTER SIXTEEN

Fourteen Hours Earlier

When Gavin saw the news that morning, his name smeared across the headlines next to Aaron's, his brain shut down. It took several minutes of staring blankly at the scrolling text at the bottom of the screen, to kickstart his thoughts.

He shook his head, to clear the cobwebs. He needed to call Aaron. As he reached for his phone, it rang. "Yeah?" The moment he answered, he suspected he should have been more cautious.

"Gavin, love. I know what you said last time we spoke, but give me thirty seconds before you hang up." It was the agent who left him a message a few days ago. If she actually remembered what he'd said, she wouldn't have called.

"Thirty. Twenty-nine. Twenty-eight."

She laughed. "I'll talk fast. You're about to get hot. As in *scorching*. Lighting screens on fire. More scalding than you were as a teenager. You give me the word, and I'll get you in front of whatever studio and director you want."

"Then you misheard me last time we spoke." He kept his tone pleasant, light, and superficial, to match hers. "I'm not an actor anymore. I retired. I don't do that. *No.*"

"I don't think you understand." A hint of condescension leaked into her voice.

Gavin's phone beeped with another call. A glance told him it was Aaron. A good reminder he needed to get this woman off the phone and cement in her head it was a waste of time to contact him. Then he could talk to Aaron. "I understand just fine. You're looking to represent someone. To use their name and career, to spin your own up. I'm not that person."

"I'll be straight with you." The cheer and lilt vanished from her voice. "When that sale happened a few years ago, it turned venture capital and Silicon Valley on their respective asses. It redefined how investments work in tech. Now, not only is it back in the spotlight, but also *you* were responsible for it. The guy who broke hearts every time he smiled at the camera. You could play yourself, in your own biopic. The pitch for this is huge. You set your price. Name your screenplay writer. Pick your co-stars. If we hop on it while it's fresh in people's minds, have an announcement out in the next two weeks while the news is still fresh, this entire deal is yours to call. Again."

A temptation he didn't want to acknowledge surged inside. The desire to negotiate with her. To ask why he should work with her and not another agent, and then start shopping deals. The impulse struggled to be heard.

You don't have to be polite to her.

Was that really what this was about? Being

nice? No. It was more. A part of him wanted to follow this thread and see where it went.

Down the toilet, along with your relationship.

"I'm not interested. Don't call me again." The words were harder to say than he expected, and they left a bitter taste in his mouth.

What was going on with his head? He wasn't interested in returning to the big screen. Even— especially not—to play a fictionalized version of himself. So why was it so tempting to explore the option? To see if the agent was right and this was his big second break. He needed to banish any doubt and call Aaron back.

His phone rang again, and an unknown number flashed on the screen. He was popular today. "Gavin Jackson."

"Gavin, hi. Ralph Wolfram with Wolfram VC. Do you have a few minutes?"

A venture capital firm? What the hell? "Now's not a great time."

"I completely understand. Tell you what— I'll leave you my number, and when you've got a few minutes, give me a ring. Just promise me you'll remember I called you first, if the offers start rolling in."

"Yeah. Sure. I'll do that." Gavin disconnected before Ralph could give him any contact information.

Too weird. Unformed thoughts buzzed in Gavin's head like a swarm of gnats. Dense. Irritating. Too tiny to bat away. He needed to rattle them loose. He tried to call Aaron and went straight to voicemail.

Take a shower, then try again. Simple

enough.

The hot water sluicing over him helped bring his jumbled mind under control, and by the time he'd dressed and stepped back into the living room, his head was much clearer. Until he saw his phone. Five missed calls, all with new messages—two from Ralph, making sure Gavin had his contact info, another from a second VC, and then a couple more talent agents.

At least he was instantly popular, the sarcasm oozed from his thoughts. Was Aaron putting up with this kind of bullshit? No. Because Aaron went through it the first time it happened, when everyone thought he was behind the sale. At the time, Gavin was happy to melt into the shadows and let Aaron take credit. Hell, it was Gavin's idea that he do so.

And it was the smart way to go. So why was he itching to call those agents back?

It didn't matter. He wasn't going to. He set his phone to *Do Not Disturb* for the next twelve hours and left it on the nightstand. Then he grabbed his Clark Kent disguise and walked out the front door.

A short while later, he approached the reception desk at Aaron's firm. The assistant flashed him a warm smile. "I'm sorry," she said. "All the partners are in a meeting and have asked not to be interrupted. Do you want to wait in his office?"

Gavin shook his head. "Don't worry about it. I'll catch up with him later."

He'd go get coffee. Kill a little time. Hole up in the back corner of their favorite diner, watch whatever the TVs were playing, and ignore the rest of the world.

The place was mostly empty when Gavin got there. Nine-thirty on a Friday morning was that point when it was a little too late to dally before work, but not quite late enough to cut out early for lunch.

The waitress grabbed him a coffee, and he settled in to relax. CNN played on the TV, subtitles scrolling by, meshing and clashing with the ticker at the bottom of the screen.

His and Aaron's pictures filled the square to the right of the anchor's head, and Gavin clenched his jaw. Why the fuck did people care so much? This was L.A.—half the people in the city were famous for one reason or another. Most of them didn't make the CNN business hour, though. Not like this.

He was too fidgety to sit still. He tossed a few bills on the table and left. His feet carried him wherever they wanted. Gavin was too wrapped up in questions, to pay attention to where he was going or how long it took. Why was he so bothered that the news was out, besides the fact that he and Aaron worked to keep Gavin's name out of the deal in the first place? Come to think of it, who was telling people the whole story? An exposé, years after the fact, seemed odd for an event most people had forgotten about.

And why was Gavin so hung up on the whole thing? He didn't want to tell that woman *no* this morning, the same way he hated to turn down fan requests. Because that response had been drilled into him since childhood.

As he roamed the city, that answer didn't sit right. He liked acting. He'd go back to it if it weren't for the crowds and the constant demand for him to be *on*, even when he wasn't in front of the camera. He'd never figured out how to be someone else on screen but himself after hours.

A growl rolled through his stomach. He'd skipped breakfast. It should be late enough for lunch by now. He glanced around at his surroundings and figured out where he was. There was a bar nearby that had decent burgers and should be playing ESPN. That would reduce the odds of seeing himself on TV.

He found the place a few minutes later. It was as empty inside as the diner had been. Was it earlier than he thought? The host seated him, and his waitress stopped at his table.

"Hey, hon. Start you off with something to drink? Coke? Tea? Something off the tap?" She looked five years younger than him, but her practiced smile and tone implied she'd been doing this for decades.

He supposed her job wasn't too much different from any actor's. Did pasting on the fakeness for real people eat at her the way it did him? "Actually, do you have bottled Sapporo? And a cheeseburger, medium rare."

"You got it." She turned away.

"Hang on. Do you have the time?"

She pulled her phone from her back pocket. "Almost three."

"Thanks." No wonder his feet hurt.

She brought his beer and set it on a cardboard coaster. As he stared at the condensation dripping down the glass, his promise to Aaron, to not drink again, echoed in his thoughts. *It's always about keeping Aaron happy.* The bitter thought caught

Gavin off guard. Of course it was. They were a couple.

The discordant ideas clashed inside. He tipped the bottle back and finished the drink in a few swallows, to silence the confusion. It didn't work. He waved down the waitress and ordered another.

He finished his lunch, but his second beer sat untouched in front of him. He could be considering calling the agent back because he needed a change. Something new to focus on. The offer from the VCs didn't tempt him, though. He wasn't interested in deciding other people's futures or signing checks. He wouldn't mind working behind the scenes again, the way he did with the original company. Maybe on a project like Cynthia's.

I should call her. Apologize for the other night. Or use the excuse to say *hi*. He reached for his phone. He'd left it at home, to escape. Which meant Aaron couldn't get a hold of him either. Speaking of Aarons—maybe Gavin should get home soon.

The thought surged with another wave of acidic bitterness he didn't understand. He took a sip of his drink and cringed. *Warm.*

He should vacate this seat before the place filled up for the night.

His wandering took him to a nearby park. He grabbed a bench and watched. People walked their dogs and jogged. As the evening faded and the sun set, a few couples walked past. No one gave him a second glance. He was a random guy, sitting to the side of the path. It was nice. So why was part of him screaming, *Look at me, damn it*?

He sat there long after it was dark, until no

one else strolled the grounds. It was probably time to go home. On the way, he passed a digital bank sign. The time flashed *10:45*. A lot later than he thought. Oops.

He reached home, unlocked the condo door, and pushed in. "Honey, I'm home."

"Where the fuck were you?" Aaron stepped into the living room.

The looming tension of the day spilled out, like a lanced boil. "Walking. Thinking." Gavin let an edge leak into his reply.

"So you just vanish for a day, without a word, on a day like today?" Dark circles hung under Aaron's eyes, and the lines in his forehead looked permanently etched. He stalked closer and wrinkled his nose. "Have you been drinking?"

Fuck. It never ended. Gavin wasn't a child who needed watching over twenty-four-seven. "No."

"Then where the fuck have you been?"

"Walking. Thinking. Why does it matter?"

Aaron's scowl slipped, leaving exhaustion in its place. "I needed you here."

"To remind me that this is a no-good, very-bad thing that happened today?" Gavin felt a sliver of guilt at reacting the way he was, but didn't want to reel himself in.

Aaron turned away and sank into the closest easy chair. "They forced me out of the firm. I wanted you here because… I wanted you here. No other reason."

"Oh." Gavin felt like a colossal shit. "I didn't mean to worry you or leave you alone. I should have been here. Is there anything I can do?"

"Not go out again tonight?" Aaron's laugh was forced.

"Of course. And whatever else you need. I'm sorry." Guilt swelled inside, mingling with resentment Gavin couldn't justify. But it was still there. Aaron wasn't asking for much; he never had. So why couldn't Gavin shake this feeling?

CHAPTER SEVENTEEN

Cynthia knocked on Aaron and Gavin's door and waited. She'd seen the news on Friday. The big *scandal* everyone said changed everything. She didn't see how. What happened, regardless of who perpetrated it. Apparently the rest of the world didn't see it that way. She'd tried to call Aaron that day, but when he didn't answer, she figured he was doing damage control.

They were supposed to meet Monday—today—and it should be the perfect time to catch up. Then she saw the press release that his firm was severing ties with him, and when she got to their office half an hour ago, she was told he was finishing his work at home.

He could have let her know.

Gavin answered, and his friendly smile chased away some of her irritation. Shadows lingered behind his gaze, but that was to be expected.

"How are you holding up?" she asked.

He shrugged. "Fielding calls from talent agents and VC firms. It's an odd sensation to be so popular again." He stepped aside. "But you're not here to see me."

"No." It would be nice if she was, but that wasn't a feeling she could afford to acknowledge. "I do wish I were here for different reasons."

"It is what it is. Aaron's in the office. Across from the bedroom." Gavin nodded down the hallway.

Cynthia wanted to give him a huge hug or something and tell him it would be all right. That felt wildly inappropriate. She settled for squeezing his fingers as she walked by. "Thanks."

He gripped her hand tighter, and she turned back to face him. He searched her face, then shook his head. "Go. Work. Have fun."

"Not phrases that usually go together, but okay." She tried not to read too much into the interaction as she strolled down the hall. She paused in the office doorway.

Aaron sat in front of a computer, tapping his fingers on the keyboard but not compressing the keys.

"Did you forget something?" She meant to tease, but her irritation slid in.

He looked up, eyes wide, and took a moment to focus on her face. "Cyn. Fuck. I meant to call you, but every time I reached for the phone, something interrupted. I was going to see if you wanted to cancel today."

"A warning would have been nice." Yeah, she couldn't do kind. "Not about the meeting, though I wasted a bit of time this morning, tracking you down."

"What, then?"

And the rant that had been bubbling inside since she heard Friday's news spilled forward. "You were willing to withhold funding from me. You threatened to drop your consideration, because of a maybe-but-not-really issue with my former business partner. A problem I had a plan to handle. Something I had under control. And the entire time, you were sitting on top of something like this? Hypocrite much?" That came out harsher than she wanted. Apparently she did see the issue with what he'd done.

It wasn't just the business aspect of things, though that bothered her. The fact that he lied to *her* settled under her skin. It forced her to acknowledge they weren't friends or anything other than mild acquaintances, although she'd let herself believe otherwise. That was her mistake, but it was easier to take it out on Aaron.

He raked shaky fingers through his hair. God. He looked worse than Gavin. She should have been nicer. "I'm sorry," he said. "If you'd like to sever ties, Liz offered to buy out your investment. A lot of my clients are taking my former partners up on similar options. If you'd like to do the same, I don't blame you."

The proposal dug deep, burrowing a hole she didn't like in her chest, until something inside snapped. "So first you lie to me, and then you try to shrug me off on someone else? Someone who passed on my idea the first time around?"

"I'm giving you the option of moving on. I'd rather keep working with you, but if you've got an issue with the news, there are ways out that will protect you and your IP."

This wasn't the Aaron she met a few short weeks ago. He was tired. Surrendering. She didn't like it. It didn't seem like him. Then again, what did she know? "I don't want a way out." She let the words flow without thought. "I want you to feel bad about keeping this from me, and I know that's not professional, but fuck it." Not what she intended to say, but it felt good to have it out there.

"I never meant… The story you know has been our reality for so long, I didn't think to say otherwise. I'm sorry."

"You should be." She struggled to hang onto her self-righteousness with him looking so defeated.

He gave her a dry smile. "If you stay with me, it won't look good for you. It'll mar your options for gathering other investors."

"I'm not in this to keep collecting funds until the company is ready to burst. I don't want to play that game or build an impressive platform worthy of a billion-dollar IPO. I'm trying to get my business off the ground and keep it solvent until it's making enough to grow on its own. You're offering me a way to do that. Or you were. Is that still the case?"

Some of the lines vanished from his face. "Yes. Nothing's changed except the name on the doorplate, if you're still interested in going down this path."

"You gave me a chance when no one else would. I like what we're doing together, and—damn it—you can't back out now because of something stupid like a little bad publicity." She moved further into the room.

Humor leaked into his smile. "Then we'd better finish the paperwork and due diligence." He gestured to a chair. "Unless you've got more to get off your chest, we should get going."

She settled into the empty seat. "That's better. I think we left off with past financial statements."

They dove into work, which, with Aaron, was a lot more enjoyable than financial statements should be.

"Have you always lived in L.A.?" Aaron asked.

"I grew up in Yuba City. After college, Emily and I moved to San Jose, because that's where the tech jobs are. And after she moved out, this seemed like it might be a better place to find clients."

"I'm glad you ended up here."

The sincerity in the simple comment heated her cheeks. "Me too."

The conversation shifted back to numbers, until Aaron said, "We stayed in Grass Valley for a few months, when I was a kid. It might as well be a different planet, compared to here."

"I can't argue with that." Nostalgia tickled Cynthia's senses. "Emily loved to go anywhere that wasn't home. When we were in high school, she used to pick a direction and just drive. We even wound up in Nevada a few times. It didn't matter to her where we went, as long as it was somewhere else."

"What about you?"

Cynthia tried to puzzle out his meaning but couldn't. "What do you mean?"

"That story. You went because Emily wanted to. What about you?"

She wasn't sure what he was getting at. "She didn't drag me against my will or anything. I still had fun. And we did lots of things I wanted to as well. It wasn't a one-way street."

"I didn't mean to imply otherwise. I'm just curious what those things were that you picked. What was your favorite pastime?"

Cynthia stalled on the question. She wasn't used to talking about herself like this. Superficial stuff? That was normal. The random flings she substituted for relationships didn't care about more. With her clients, it wasn't about her, and she and Emily already knew everything about each other. Or they used to. "Ice cream? The bookstore? Movies?" she chuckled. "It makes me sound kind of boring."

"Not at all. I think it sounds fantastic."

Talk shifted back to her business's money and tripped from one random topic to the next.

"Wow." Aaron's exclamation caught her off guard. "It's almost eleven. Do you want to take a break?"

She blinked and rubbed her eyes. She hadn't realized how weary her brain was until he said something. "A break sounds great."

They wandered toward the kitchen. She didn't see Gavin, but it felt impolite to actively seek him out if he wasn't in plain view.

"Do you want something to drink?" Aaron approached the fridge.

"Water. Lots of ice." It was cool inside, but the sun beat through the glass of the balcony door. When she showed up this morning, she wasn't sure what she was going to do or say. The last couple of hours made her decision to stick with Aaron feel right. "There's a huge perk to working here, instead of in an office."

"Oh?" He handed her a glass and joined her

on the patio.

Before following, she shrugged off her suit jacket and draped it over the back of a chair. "It's a lot more comfortable and casual here." She'd feel odd wearing the sleeveless top in a more professional environment. She stepped up next to him on the cement and let her gaze travel over the city below. It was a gorgeous view, and she could see all the way to the mountains.

"I won't be offended if you want to wear something more comfortable tomorrow." Aaron stood close enough she could distinguish the heat of his arm near hers from the morning sunshine. "You've already made the right impressions."

She heard another set of footsteps from behind, and a second later, the glass door slid shut. There was Gavin. She half expected a joke like, *Or you could wear nothing at all.*

"I owe you an apology." Gavin's voice was missing its usual cheer.

An ache settled in her bones, to hear him sounding less than on-top. At the same time, she liked knowing he was comfortable enough around her to show her this side of himself. It was an odd contradiction. She turned to face him. "It's done and over." She wanted the words to be an all-encompassing kind of thing. As in, there was no reason to apologize. No need to bring up the other night at the club. It wasn't as if that part of their relationship would continue.

She couldn't force out the specific words, and despite the insistence inside, she wasn't sure if she wanted him to read more into her statement or not.

Something cold dripped between her breasts, and she gasped. It was the moisture from the edges of her glass.

Gavin hadn't replied, and she looked up to find him watching her. Gaze locked on hers, he drew a finger up her chest, along the fallen drop of water. Despite the summer heat, a pleasant chill raced over her, raising goosebumps.

"You didn't deserve what I did. I interrupted a perfectly incredible evening." He dragged his damp finger along her bottom lip, and her mouth parted in a silent sigh.

"I think the moment was lost." Aaron's strained words came from behind her.

She didn't know if it was stress or desire lining his voice.

Gavin continued to watch Cynthia, making her pulse race. "I have a good idea where to find it." There was no mistaking the undercurrent in his tone—apology, mixed with need. He leaned closer, breath hot on her cheek and then her ear, but never made contact. "I know this isn't a crowded dance floor, but I promise not to interrupt this time. I'll sit back and watch, though I can't swear I'll be quiet."

Want spilled through her, carried on a wave of images and his intoxicating scent. The fantasy of screwing Aaron while Gavin watched teased her thoughts. Gavin's closeness amplified each flash in her mind, until the fantasy clenched in her belly and traveled lower, to thrum between her thighs.

Hell, she liked what he was implying. There was a problem, though, and logic chose that moment to rear its nasty head. For all the justifications she'd made in the past, if she did this again, she wouldn't be able to pretend it was meaningless. Her reaction this morning to Aaron's deception—thinking he owed her anything more than professional courtesy—was proof she was dangerously close to losing the detachment she needed.

"Well?"

She felt more than heard Gavin's whisper as it caressed her skin. She swore the whole world held its breath, waiting for her answer. She certainly did. She reached deep, past lust and want and the craving for Aaron and Gavin's touch, and grabbed resolve she didn't know she had. "No. That's not a good idea."

"All right." Gavin stepped away. Despite the casual words, he was scowling.

"She's right." Aaron's agreement bolstered her decision. "And the two of us need to get back to work."

"It was amazing"—Cynthia looked at Gavin—"but we all knew it was only temporary."

"You don't owe anyone an explanation," Aaron said.

"Nope." Gavin's smile was brighter than the sun and hurt more to look at. "Bad idea on my part. The past was just fun. And in the past. It didn't mean anything. I'll let you get back to what you were doing."

Cynthia hated how clipped his words were and that she was responsible for it. At the same time, resentment tingled inside that he made her feel bad for saying *no*.

CHAPTER EIGHTEEN

Gavin knew, deep in his bones and all through him, that Cynthia had a right to turn down his playful offer. That didn't stop the rejection from lingering where reason should be. He made himself scarce while Aaron and Cynthia finished working for the day. And even after she left.

He was busy enough anyway. It seemed as though someone new called with *the offer of a lifetime* every couple of hours. Another agent or venture capitalist or technical recruiter.

He gave the recruiters his attention. Since he'd enjoyed creating the thing the first time around, it seemed like a good chance to see if someone would let him dig in and get technical again. No one offered what he was looking for, though.

Each time Gavin's phone rang, Aaron tried to hide a frown.

The tension in the house grew to oppressive levels, and by Thursday morning, Gavin was tempted to toss his phone off the balcony.

It might make a more satisfying *crunch* if he threw it in the blender.

He agreed to meet with the one headhunter

who had a reasonable-sounding position.

Stepping out of the house was more of a relief than Gavin wanted to admit. The job he'd been sold on—Creative Control and Design over a new artificial-intelligence algorithm—was nothing like the Vice President position pitched when he sat down for lunch. He told the recruiter *thanks, but no thanks,* and sent the guy on his way.

Gavin wasn't ready to go home yet. He took a seat at the bar and stared at the TV, not registering what was playing.

The bartender set a shot glass of amber liquid in front of him. Gavin waved it away. "I didn't order this."

"It's on me." A blonde took the stool next to him. Her suit—silk blouse, pinstriped jacket and matching slacks—made Gavin think she'd escaped an afternoon of corporate torture. And didn't remind him in the least of Cynthia.

As long as she wasn't there to offer him a job he didn't want or talk him into reviving his career, he was grateful for the company. He gave her a warm smile. "I can't accept a drink from a stranger."

She extended her hand. "Amelia."

"Gavin." He gripped her palm. Her skin was cool and smooth against his, chasing away the clouds that had lingered all week.

"Now we're not strangers anymore." She lifted her glass. "Cheers?"

Fuck it. He was tired of doing what was expected of him. He clinked his drink against hers, then downed the tequila in a single swallow. It burned smooth and hot, sliding down his throat. That felt and tasted better than it should. Like visiting an old friend he'd ignored for way too long. He waved the bartender over. "Two more."

* * * *

Aaron wrapped up work for the day. The only good thing about him going his separate way from the firm was that shutting a few windows on his computer was easier than walking home. Not that the latter took much effort. Maybe he'd take tomorrow off. In the last week, he'd lost board seats with almost every one of his investments, signed most of their contracts over to former partners, and been told at least a couple of times to go fuck himself.

The conversation he'd had with Cynthia on Monday was rainbows and unicorns, compared to the way things went with pretty much everyone else. She was the only person who opted to stay with him.

He was exhausted, mentally and physically. A three-day weekend would give him time to find his mojo again. He'd land on his feet—he always did— but right now he needed to temporarily lift some of the weight from his shoulders.

The front door clicked open. Before he could call out and ask Gavin how the interview went, he heard, "Honey, we're home."

We? Aaron padded into the living room. When he saw the woman half-standing, half-leaning against Gavin, he froze.

"Hello." She waved. Pink flushed her cheeks, and she seemed to have an infatuation with chewing on her bottom lip.

Gavin made a sweeping gesture with his arm. "Amelia, this is the love of my life, Aaron."

"I've heard a bunch about you." Amelia giggled. "You're as sexy as he says."

Aaron processed a couple of thoughts in a few-seconds span. Amelia bore an eerie resemblance to Cynthia. Not so much they could be confused in decent lighting, but enough they might be cousins. And Gavin was drunk.

"It's barely five." Aaron couldn't keep the reproach from his voice.

Gavin laughed. "So it's not just five o'clock somewhere; it's five o'clock *here*. I was telling Amelia how much fun we like to have, and she's curious."

"Very." Amelia's flush deepened.

Aaron had a suspicion they were talking about sex, but he didn't like to assume. "Fun with what?"

"Making Amelia the filling in an Oreo cookie. Since our last cookie is done with us."

Aaron winced at the disdain in Gavin's voice. "Cyn's my business partner. Not a cookie."

"Who's that?" Amelia asked.

"No one important." Gavin kissed her on the cheek. "Not with you here. She got bored and moved on, and that's fine with me."

This was better than any other time in the past. The sarcastic thought rushed through Aaron's head. Gavin wasn't just drunk and childish, he was also acting like he'd been dumped. By Cynthia. *Fabulous*. The realization soured inside Aaron, mingling with everything else bitter.

"It's lovely to meet you." He closed the distance to them and wrapped an arm around Amelia's waist. "I'll call you a ride, and you can get home safely."

She pouted. "I want to stay here."

"Don't be a spoil sport," Gavin said.

Aaron flicked through the app on his phone to grab a car for Amelia. Seconds later he pocketed the device. "Silver Accord. They'll be here in ten minutes. You'll see them better if you wait in the lobby."

He hated to hustle the woman out the door, but he was millimeters from losing his shit, and he didn't want any witnesses.

Gavin kissed Amelia on the cheek. "Sorry, love. I didn't know Oscar the Grouch was here. I'll call you."

"Okay." The door closed behind her.

"What the fuck is your problem?" Gavin whirled on him.

Aaron stared back in disbelief. How dare he pull any sort of self-righteous bullshit? "Do you want a list? Let's start with how drunk you are."

"Not nearly as much as I need to be, to put up with this. She was a nice girl, and you were rude."

So many emotions churned inside Aaron in an acidic cocktail, he didn't know which to focus on. Disbelief would be the least painful, but hurt and anger rose to the top. "I'm sorry I couldn't paste on a fake smile for a random stranger. Maybe if you'd brought home a bottle of whatever's racing through your veins, it would help. It's been a really shitty week, and I'm not in the mood."

"That doesn't mean you have to take it out on me."

"I'd rather lean on you for support. You know, like what I've given you for over a decade. You're not making that easy, though." Aaron was surprised at thoughts he didn't realize were there until the words hit his tongue. "That's all I've wanted from you for the past few days."

"*This* week." Gavin spat the words. "And last week, it was for me to pretend I wasn't being hounded by fans—"

Aaron couldn't believe that was thrown back in his face. "You mean that pack in the restaurant? Or the club? When I tried to pull you away?"

"And two months ago, it was, *just promise me you won't drink anymore*. And five years ago, it was, *I can't stay with you if you can't give up the coke*. And ten years ago, it was, *Acting is killing you. Walk away. For me*. And Monday, it was, *Don't hit on my business partner*."

Aaron almost choked on the venom flung in his direction. "Holy fuck. You're serious."

"What I'm serious about is that being with me seems to make you miserable. If you hate it so much, why do you stick around?"

"I *stick around* because I love you. And for a long time, I convinced myself that it didn't matter that you refused to deal with whatever is haunting you, because it was in the past." Aaron wasn't putting up with this. "You can't blame your life and your decisions on everyone else. Saying you stopped drinking for me, instead of you. Saying Cyn destroyed a relationship... You didn't have a fucking relationship with her. Not like that. Insisting your upbringing is the reason you have to stop and smile for every fucking fan who wants your autograph. If you don't want any of that, don't do it."

"Great advice. I made it that far on my own. Hence the afternoon of tequila shots with a gorgeous blonde who wanted to be there and wasn't flirting with me for your approval and money."

Aaron clenched his fist and a growl slipped out without his permission. If this was anyone else, he'd deck them for a comment like that. "Don't take your childish fucking insecurities out on Cynthia. This isn't about her."

"Fine." Despite the defiance in Gavin's voice, some of his swagger vanished. "Let's focus on you and me. You wouldn't be anywhere financially, without me. You were pulling cheap-ass tricks on a back lot, and you'd be in jail now if we hadn't met."

The reminder hurt. It dug under the insecurity Aaron never managed to shake, that he was his father's son. "That may be true, and I'm willing to face that reality. Can you do the same?"

"Admit you're nothing without me?"

"Confront your fucking flaws and fix them."

Gavin rolled his eyes. "There's nothing wrong with me, except that you keep telling me I'm broken."

"Other people may buy that bullshit, but I don't." Aaron saw where this was headed, and a sliver of terror told him to back down. To make their relationship right before they said things they couldn't take back. Except they'd passed that point, and he hadn't realized they were near snapping until it happened. "The one thing I can thank my father for? I can spot a bad con from a mile away. And the lies you tell yourself? They ooze to the surface. *You* don't even believe them."

"Fuck you." Gavin spun, walked out the door, and slammed it behind him.

Aaron leaned against the wall for support, as his legs threatened to give out. He let out a long gasp and clenched his fists so hard, his nails dug into his palms. He itched to go after Gavin. To chase him down and figure out what just happened, and make things right.

Not tonight. The thought looped in his head until it took hold. That hadn't worked in the past, and the things that had come out… Aaron was too raw to go through Round Two. Besides, the alcohol didn't invent what wasn't there; it only made it easier to admit what was.

"Not tonight." Aaron spoke the words aloud and let them echo in the empty condo.

CHAPTER NINETEEN

I can't make our meeting today. Send me the rest of your paperwork as you have it, but consider yourself funded. Third board position is yours to fill.

Cynthia stared at the brief email from Aaron and reread it a third time to make sure she wasn't missing something. She understood the first part. He had a lot going on right now; it made sense he'd have to cancel an appointment or two.

But halting the due diligence was odd. And the board position… She'd assumed he'd give that to Gavin or hold onto it for another financial partner, to secure veto rights if she and Aaron reached an impasse.

It was best not to dwell on it. She had work to do, and this way she didn't have to see Aaron and Gavin too much. Since Emily and Paul walked out of her life, she'd thrown herself into work and getting funding, in order to ignore that she was lonely. Aaron and Gavin were just another way to fill that void.

The empty pit in her gut argued there was more to it than that, but loneliness could play cruel tricks.

The rest of her Friday passed without

incident, though she didn't get as much work done as she hoped. Every time her phone buzzed, she grabbed it, hoping for something from Aaron.

She closed up her office and headed home. Maybe she should go out tonight. Dancing or drinking. *Not alone. That's no fun.*

Unless she met someone. The idea hit her thoughts with a dull *thud*. Home it was.

Her weekend wasn't as pleasant as she wanted. Saturday she called Emily and went straight to voicemail. "Hey, it's me." Cynthia kept her tone light. "Just calling to say *hi*. There's no rush to get back to me."

She went back to the office. She was set up to work from home, but it felt more official to do business from her place of business. She sifted through existing client records, wrote up ads for new job postings, and tweaked some of her code. The algorithm for matching more than two people still wasn't quite right, and now that she'd put feelers out, more of her clients were requesting the option.

Thoughts of Aaron and Gavin slammed into her. The way they treated conversation like a hacky sack. The more searing moments when things got intimate—between them and with her—hands running over bare skin and lips following. Aaron gliding a hand under her dress, to pinch a nipple. Gavin pushing her hand up the inside of her thigh, to tease her sex.

She reached for her phone, then stopped herself. It wasn't right to call them because she didn't have a social life.

She forced her attention back to her work, but

the computer took longer to return results with each new task. She'd need to upgrade some of her hardware soon. Which meant a whole new round of decisions and purchases she hadn't accounted for this early in the timeline.

By Monday morning, she needed Aaron's input on the server purchase. *You really don't*, her thoughts taunted her, as she picked up the phone. But he was a business partner. He had a say in major purchases.

She winced with each ring, and when she went to voicemail, she disconnected without leaving a message.

It wouldn't hurt to drop by the condo and ask him in person. Not because she missed him or Gavin, but sometimes an in-person meeting was a good way to keep lines of communication open.

When she reached their place, she knocked and waited. Seconds ticked away. Something clattered inside. Or was that from a neighboring place? She tapped her toes inside her shoes. She should knock again, but that pushed the limits of claiming she was here on a casual visit. Maybe… No. It was time to go. This was something that could be done with an email or a phone call or without his input at all. Why was she here?

She turned on her toe, and a latch clinked behind her.

"Hey, Cyn." Aaron's greeting was tired.

A fist clenched around her heart at the sadness filling her voice.

She whirled back to face him, her smile brighter than she intended. "Hey." Concern spread through her when she saw the lines on his face matched the exhaustion in his tone. "How are you?"

"Fine. What's up?"

She hesitated. "Do you have a few minutes to talk business?"

"Now really isn't a good time. Email it to me, and I'll look it over."

"It'll only take a few minutes." Great. Now she sounded desperate. *Leave the guy alone. Take a hint.*

Aaron sighed. "What is it?"

"I need to upgrade my servers..." She trailed off when his frown deepened.

"I trust you. You don't have to run every one of these decisions by me."

"I know. It's just that..." *Go. Now.* But she couldn't. "What's wrong?"

He shook his head. "Personal stuff. Not the kind of thing that makes for a good business conversation."

The brush-off hurt. It shouldn't, but that didn't stop the ache from filling her chest. It wasn't as though they were close. Sex and work—that was all they had. It didn't stop her from wanting to sit by his side until he was feeling better. "As long as you're talking to someone about it. Gavin, maybe?"

Aaron clenched his jaw and his nostrils flared.

"I'm-sorry-I-didn't-mean..." The words tumbled out, but she couldn't find the right ones to finish the thought.

His chuckle was clipped and dark. "I might be talking to him, if he were here. Oh, wait. That's the problem."

She should walk away and keep things professional, but she couldn't. Everything spilling from Aaron gnawed at her and filled her with the desire to help. To see him feeling better. "Let me in, and I'll listen. No judgment. No taking sides. I'm here."

"That's not going to work for me." He stepped aside anyway. "I'd rather you took *my* side." His scowl cracked, and for a moment she thought he might smile, but a shadow moved back in again.

"No deal. But I'm listening." She took a seat in one of the easy chairs in the living room.

He paced in front of her, rubbing the tips of his fingers together, gaze cast at the floor.

She let that continue for a moment before saying, "What's going on?"

Aaron looked let out a long breath. "We had a fight Thursday night, and I haven't seen him since. He's not answering his phone. Not that I tried very hard before Sunday."

"What happened Sunday?"

Aaron looked at her, pain echoing in his eyes. "Concern won out over spite and anger."

"What was the fight about?" She didn't miss the way he glossed over the details, or his hesitation, as if he wanted to say more.

"Everything. The same old things, but with a new and cruel twist. I'm not supportive enough. He's under a lot of pressure, and it drives his addictions. I accused him of a lot of things I probably shouldn't have. I… I got tired of being the responsible one."

"If you said it in the heat of the moment, it's

been gnawing at you long enough to work its way out." She measured her answer carefully. Not taking sides would be difficult if she wanted to comfort him, but she only had his side of the story.

That wasn't completely true. She saw the tension in the club, and the way both Aaron and Gavin reacted. If their fight was related to things like that, she had a bit more sympathy for Aaron. "You reached a point where you felt you had to do something different," she said.

"I said horrible things." His voice wavered, as if he didn't quite believe himself.

"The two of you can work this out."

"How?" Of course he'd ask that.

"If I had that answer—if it were that easy—things probably wouldn't have gotten so bad in the…" As she recited the stock answer, a reality settled deep inside. She'd never believed the really big rough patches could be worked through. It was easy to go through the motions and repeat the psychology she learned in college, but deep down inside, she assumed all romantic relationships were doomed to fail. The realization chewed at her senses and stung her soul. For the first time since she could remember, she wanted to be wrong about that. She wanted Aaron and Gavin to make it through whatever this was.

God, she was stupid to try and push Paul and Emily together. The numbers, the code, the matchmaking software—it said the two would work. But the chemistry was never there.

"Cyn?" Aaron's question penetrated her rambling thoughts. "Wouldn't have gotten that bad in the first place? Is that what you were saying?"

She nodded. "Sorry. I was just thinking what the two of you have is so real. I can see that, and I barely know you. That kind of passion will rub the wrong way sometimes, but you can't give up. *He* can't give up."

Aaron shook his head. "I don't know if we have a lot of options. I hate to sound fatalistic, but this feels different. I don't know if there's any going back for either of us."

She reached for his hand and squeezed his fingers, but had no wise words or comfort to share.

*

Gavin lay in bed in his hotel room, staring at the ceiling. It was Tuesday evening. Six days since the argument with Aaron. Almost a week since he'd been home. He knew that without question, because even though he'd drunk enough over that time frame to drown himself, he still remembered.

He remembered everything he said and Aaron's retorts. He tried to summon the rage he had during the fight, but it was gone. Drifted away hours or days ago, leaving him with an empty pit inside.

He got up and ambled into the bathroom, to splash cold water on his face. He paused in front of the mirror, and his reflection stared back at him with bloodshot eyes.

Habit and longing begged him to go back to Aaron, but he wouldn't. He couldn't. Not after the things that were said. The accusations thrown at Gavin.

Maybe Aaron had a point. You need to be the one to change.

Gavin hated that voice. It sounded like Aaron and got loud every time sobriety sank in. "Maybe people need to understand where I'm coming from and stop making unrealistic demands," he told the mirror-image. His voice echoed off tile, taunting him.

Way to pass the blame to someone else. Again.

Rage poured through him. "Shut *up*." He smashed his fist into the mirror. The sound of shattering glass, along with the pain shooting through his knuckles, jarred him out of his head and back to reality. A fractured version of him stared back. It seemed appropriate.

He needed a drink. And to wash the blood from his knuckles. He was out of liquor, and the hotel bar sucked, so he'd take care of the wound first, and then head out. Get laid. Get wasted. Maybe find something stronger, to help him forget.

He stripped off his boxers and stepped into the shower, where he stood under the stream, barely noticing as it slid from cold to scalding.

If he went to Aaron and demanded they make things work, Aaron would listen.

It won't be that easy this time.

Fuck. The nagging voice had a point. And he needed to get out of his head before he went nuts. He shut off the water, and ran a towel over himself. His skin was still damp when he pulled on slacks and a button-down. He was going out. As himself. To the one place he wanted to be recognized—the club where he was guaranteed to get in because of his past star status, and he could score… well, anything really.

He headed downstairs and had the concierge call him a taxi. Tonight could be a good night for X.

Because you need to feel more intensely? Are you sure that's smart?

He growled inwardly at the pseudo-Aaron voice. Coke, then.

Do you think I'll shut up if you're wired like that?

Fine. Heroin. He'd stayed away from the addictive drugs in the past—alcohol had sharp enough hooks—but tonight he wasn't picky. He wanted something to make him numb.

That sounds like the perfect solution.

Great. Now he was being sarcastic with himself.

The ride to the club seemed to take forever but was only about twenty minutes. Even on a weeknight, there was a line to get in. Gavin didn't wait. He flashed the doorman a smile, and a moment later he was stepping into a different world where the reality of outside didn't matter. There was only *now*.

* * * *

When Gavin pried his eyes open Wednesday, the sun still shone through his east-facing window, and the clock by the bed said it was ten. Fuck. Sobriety sucked. His headache and dry eyes weren't due to a hangover, because the strongest thing he took last night was an extra dose of Tylenol PM.

Because that fucking Aaron-voice wouldn't shut up, Gavin came back here alone.

Right. Blame me for your faults, when I'm not even there.

Gavin pressed his palms to his eyes until all he saw were a million pinpricks dotting the blackness. This needed to stop. What was he supposed to do? He couldn't go home after what happened. There was too much he'd done—

The words started to form, but he couldn't let himself think them. He could return to acting. Then he'd have the fun to go with the drinking.

Fuck this. Fuck it all. He grabbed his phone and dialed a number he hadn't touched in years.

"This is Heather." The woman on the other end was so chipper, it made Gavin wince.

At the same time, he was grateful she answered. "It's Gavin Jackson."

"No shit. It's really you? It's been ages."

He didn't know if he was about to do the right thing, but something needed to give. He had to try something different, and maybe piss off the voice in his head enough to shut it up. "I know. But I'm hoping I can put you on retainer for a few weeks."

"Weeks. Months. Whatever you need, you know I'll do it."

"First you have to swear that *none* of what we're about to discuss gets out until tomorrow morning. Not a single bit of it can leak, regardless of who else is involved. No one can know where I'm going or what I'm doing."

"You know what I'm capable of." There was no hesitation in her voice. Heather was the best publicist he'd ever met. It wasn't just her knack for making things public, it was also her insane skill at keeping them quiet and under wraps until it was time to do otherwise.

He smiled his first genuine smile in days. "I do. And that's why I called." If his world was going to crumble either way, he was going to step up, own the direction it fell, and break and reassemble it the way he wanted.

CHAPTER TWENTY

Aaron stared at the incoming call and Gavin's picture on the screen. Almost a week with no word. He'd strung himself from fear to anger to guilt, then back down the line in the other direction. And now Aaron couldn't take the call. Not yet. He swiped *ignore*.

Despite spending the next several hours trying to figure out what to say to Gavin, he didn't take the next two calls either. Irritation raged inside, until he thought he might scream. It was just a fight. They'd had them before and still been together for over a decade. What the fuck was wrong with him?

The internal struggle couldn't convince him to listen to the three voicemails. He went to bed that night wishing the answers were written on the wall.

He woke up to a slew of new alerts with Gavin's name. Aaron's mind twisted further in on itself. He deleted the emails unread and ignored the phone call from their lawyer. He sat in the home office, staring at the wall, willing himself to stop ignoring the world. Things needed to be dealt with. Faced. Confronted. Hiding wasn't his thing.

Thinking the words didn't make it any easier

to take action. When his phone rang, he only grabbed it because Cyn's name was on the screen. "*What*?"

"That's what I thought." Her sympathetic tone was an irritation in an already raw wound, and at the same time a salve over it. "Have you left the house since I was there?"

"Yes. I'm not a recluse. Just frustrated." Furious. Guilt-ridden. Terrifi— "What's up?"

"Meet me for coffee. Half an hour. No arguments."

"I don't—"

"Half an hour. There's a place a few blocks from your condo, so you've got plenty of time."

His brain was too battered to come up with an argument. Not that he wanted to. "I'll be there."

She was waiting and had staked out a table, when he arrived at the coffee shop. She stood as he approached, and wrapped him in a tight hug when he was close enough. Surprise froze his thoughts, but he recovered quickly and squeezed back, the gesture an amazing kind of comforting. Disappointment whispered in when she pulled away and took her seat.

She nudged a cup toward him. "Spanish latte. Emily swears they make life better. They're not as good here as the place in San Jose, but they're not bad."

"Thanks." He took a sip. Cyn was right; it was a decent drink.

The way she watched him, brows furrowed and pity in her eyes, set his teeth on edge. "How are you holding up?" she asked.

A little more frazzled. A little less sure of what to do next. Nothing worth delving into, though.

"Same as all week."

She raised her brows, mouth twisted in surprise.

"You expected I'd be doing better?" He gave a bitter laugh.

"Have you seen the headlines today?"

Fuck. "I've never had a morning in the entirety of my adult life when that question led to a good conversation. And no."

"You should."

"Or you could fucking tell me." The words came out in a sharp bark. "Did Gavin start his career again? Get arrested? Is the SEC filing an investigation into my financial dealings? *What?*" He winced at the hurt that mingled with her shock. "I'm sorry. Please tell me."

She sighed and turned her gaze to her hands. "Gavin checked himself into rehab. There was an official statement from his publicist about it." Cyn wasn't telling him everything. The hesitation in her words said she held back.

"What else?" he asked.

She clenched her hand until her knuckles turned white and her fist shook. "The press release also said… he's split from his long-time partner."

Aaron gripped the edge of the table as his world tilted on its axis. "I need to be alone." He pushed back from the table, the legs of his chair screeching on tile.

Cynthia grabbed his wrist. "Call me—or someone—when you're ready to talk."

"I will." He was already on his way out the door. He didn't dare think or feel. Was afraid the world around him might crumble if he admitted things were falling apart. He pulled out his cellphone and dialed into his voicemail.

"It's me." Gavin's recorded voice sent a shudder through him. "We need to talk. Call me back today."

Aaron gasped as an invisible hand clenched around his chest. He leaned against a nearby building, turned his gaze to the sky, and let the next message play.

"It's urgent. You need to call me before tomorrow." Gavin's tone was flat.

Aaron wasn't sure he wanted to hear the last message, but he listened anyway.

"I hoped to do this face to face." Gavin's voice was still cool. Devoid of emotion. "I should have stopped by the house before I checked myself in, but I was afraid you'd talk me out of splitting from you, or that seeing you would make me change my mind. My best hope now is that you get this before you see the news tomorrow. I can't be with you anymore. I love you, and I'm sorry."

Aaron let his arm fall limply to his side, and he stared, not processing anything. He expected chaos in his head, but he only had one thought. He needed to talk to Gavin.

The only bright spot Aaron saw in the news was that he had a pretty good idea where to find him. There was a *spa* outside the valley, a Hollywood worst-kept secret. It took about two seconds of searching for Aaron to find the number and dial.

"Sunshine Wellness and Health. May I help you?" The man who answered was sweet to the point of saccharine.

Aaron shoved everything negative aside and adopted a cheerful, direct tone. "I'm looking for Gavin Jackson. I believe he's a patient there?"

"I'm sorry. There's no one here by that name. Can I do anything else I can do for you?"

That made sense. Of course a clinic known for its high profile clients wasn't going to flinch at denying who their patients were. "That's fine, I understand. I'm looking for my partner. My name is Aaron Birch, or it may be under Murdock."

"I'm sorry. We don't have anyone on our approved visitor list under that name."

"Are you su—"

"Have a pleasant afternoon, sir."

The line went dead. Aaron ground his teeth together until his jaw ached. He should have known that wouldn't work. The place was about an hour's drive, probably longer in daytime traffic, but he'd do this in person. Show ID, put on a smile, and get what he needed.

An hour and a half later, he stood in the lobby of Sunshine Wellness and Health. "Hey." He approached the counter with a casual gait, locking away everything that churned inside. "How's it going?"

The guy at the desk gave him a painted-on smile that didn't reach his eyes. "Can I help you?"

"Absolutely. I'm Murdock Aaron Birch." He pulled out his driver's license. "How are you doing this afternoon?"

"Great." The guy's flat tone clashed with his retort. "Can I help you?"

"Here to visit. Is this where I sign in?" Aaron nudged an open binder on the counter.

The man shut the book. "No. That's for people visiting our guests."

"Which I am. I'm here to see Gavin Jackson."

"There's no one here by that name."

"Of course there's not. He wouldn't check in under his real name. But I'm on the visitor list."

The man kept his gaze on Aaron. "You're not."

"You're sure? You don't want to check the system first and verify that? Aaron's a common name."

"I have an excellent memory."

"Really?" Aaron's friendly mask slipped. "You've memorized the roster of who is and isn't allowed in?"

The guy winced. "Yes."

Aaron raised his brows.

"Look," the employee said. "If the person you're looking for were here—which I'm not confirming—you'd specifically be on the *do not permit* list. I'm going to have to ask you to leave."

"I see. Thank you." The numbness flowing through Aaron's veins was better than letting the hurt and disbelief knock him off his feet.

*

Cynthia hated being the person to deliver the news to Aaron almost as much as she hated leaving him alone after, but instinct told her she needed to give him a little space to process. She wouldn't want to be stuck in a stranger's company after something like that.

Except they weren't strangers. Or even simple business associates.

She should get back to work. There was so much to do. Each time she tried to put her head down and focus, Aaron's hurt expression flashed through her mind.

When she started this idea, both while Emily was still here and after, when it was just Cynthia, she'd put in long hours and weekends without hesitation. Now she was itching to bolt from her chair like she was hourly.

She forced herself to stick it out for the full workday. Not that she had much to show for it when five hit and she was on her way to Aaron and Gavin's.

Aaron answered with a scowl that looked etched in. "Do you ever stop working?"

She would have laughed at the question if the situation weren't so somber. "I'm not here because of work. No pretenses. I'm worried about you."

"Why?"

Her mind recoiled at the venom in his voice. "Because I care," she said.

"We're fucking business partners. Why do you give a shit about anything outside of that?"

She'd been asking herself the same question all day, and the answer was obvious now. "Besides the fact that we're human, and you deserve compassion? We're not *just* business partners. I'm not going to keep lying to myself or to you about that."

"Whatever." His tone softened, and he opened the door wider.

She strolled into his apartment and spun to face him. "It's like this. Sometimes you know a person your entire life, but you never really do. My brother and I were that way. Other times, you think you know someone, but you've kept so much hidden, the connection isn't solid. It's not as real as it could be. And then there are those people you click with. It only takes five or ten minutes of talking to them, and the spark is obvious. There's a bond there that can be more. Friendship. Love. Whatever it is, it's meant to last."

He brushed past her and dropped onto the couch with a sigh. He scrubbed his face. "What if you think you have that bond, but you're lying to yourself?"

"The two aren't mutually exclusive. The important thing is that once you recognize something is missing, you correct it, so you don't lose that long-term bond. You and I"—she bit back the *and Gavin* that wanted to make itself heard—"have that connection. The first night we met, we clicked. So yeah, we're business partners. But I consider you a friend, too—hopefully for a long time—and I'm worried about you. Which means you're going to put up with frequent visits while you work through this. If you want to talk business, and nothing else, that's fine, but if you ever want to talk about Gavin or anything else, I'm here."

"I can't talk about… him. I'd rather talk *to* him, but that doesn't seem like it will be easy. I could flood his email, but that feels a bit stalkerish. Going to the clinic probably was too, but I can't simply walk away."

"But you don't want to talk about him?"

He let out a small laugh. It was lined with melancholy, but it was a start. "No. Not yet."

"In that case, plug your ears, because I'm going to. There will be a point where he's ready to take your calls. As long as you're still waiting."

"Of course I will be. I'm not giving up on us."

"I know." And she did. There were few things she was more certain of than the fact that Gavin and Aaron belonged together. The thought rocked inside, chewing at her heart. It hurt to see them apart, and at the same time, the selfish part of her longed to have something even a fraction as beautiful as their relationship. The kind of thing she would have insisted didn't exist two months ago.

CHAPTER TWENTY-ONE

Gavin stared at the phone, willing it to give him answers.

His afternoon session with his therapist replayed in his head.

Tell me about Aaron, she'd said.

Gavin didn't think that was a good idea. He missed Aaron so bad, it left a hollow pit in his chest. But he also wasn't ready to delve into that part of his life yet. Not with the wounds so fresh.

If you have a friend who's supportive, who will listen, dial them up, the therapist told him. *You don't have to, but company from the outside will be nice. Trust me.*

So he'd asked her to get him a phone number. It wasn't hard to find. Now he looked between the paper holding the digits and the phone, trying to figure out if this was a good idea. Every bit of logic in his head said it wasn't.

Which, given his recent track record, meant he should probably do it. He dialed before he could talk himself out of it.

"Hello?" Cynthia's voice summoned a smile.

"Hey. It's Gavin. Gavin Jackson."

"As opposed to… Gavin Smith?"

He chuckled. Wow. That felt good. "Do you have a minute?"

"Yes?" Her surprise and hesitation were clear.

"It's kind of sad. I grew up with so much fame." He didn't mean to muse aloud, but she didn't cut him off. "Aaron was the only person who really knew me." Saying those words—thinking about what he and Aaron used to have—hurt more than Gavin expected. "I can't talk to him yet. I don't know anyone else who cares enough to take my call for non-business reasons. I'm not being all *woe is me*; it's the nature of the life I've led."

"So you called me."

He didn't know how to interpret her tone. "I had a feeling you'd care. You're the closest thing I have to a friend right now, though we don't know each other very well."

"I get it. I do." She sounded sincere. "And it's nice to hear from you."

Relief spread inside. That was the best thing he'd heard since he'd arrived. "Now that we have the formalities out of the way, when are you coming to visit?" He forced a teasing tone into his question. It was the nearest to normal he'd felt in weeks. Then again, Cynthia brought that out in him.

The silence that stretched over the line shattered the tentative calm. "Yeah. Visit. Whenever you'll have me."

"Don't do me any favors." The joy bled from him.

She sighed. "It's not that, but I'm processing.

Aaron…"

"I can't face him." How did Gavin think Aaron wouldn't come up? "Is he a condition?"

"No." Her answer came instantly this time. "But I won't lie to him about it."

"Are you going to offer him a transcript of our conversations?"

"No. I just want you to know up front that I want to see the two of you back together. Friendship isn't my only motive."

The statement should have made Gavin wince, but as much of him was grateful for it as not. "That's fair. Friends, huh?"

"Aren't we?"

"I hope so." The tension drained from his neck. "What I'm hearing is I'll see you Saturday afternoon?"

"Give me an address, and I'll be there at one."

Gavin couldn't fight his smile as he hung up the phone. When was the last time a conversation was that easy and no-strings with Aaron? The question erased his good mood.

* * * *

Everything inside Aaron's heart ached. He'd never realized this kind of pain was real. It had been two weeks, and the wounds were as raw as when he and Gavin fought last. Now he sat across from Cyn, trying to quell a fresh surge of agony. "I've been trying to find a way in to see him, for… well… since I heard the news," he said.

"I know."

"And he calls you out of the blue and insists you visit."

She shrugged. "I'm sure he would have taken a *no* if I said it, but he was persuasive. You know how he is."

"I do." He could almost hear Gavin in his head. Never asking, just assuming Cyn would say *yes*.

"I said I'd only see him if he understood I want to see the two of you back together. And I mean that."

"And he was okay with that?"

"He didn't protest."

"Good, I guess?" Bitterness mingled with hope. It was an unpleasant combination. He didn't miss the way Gavin and Cyn got along—that spark the first time they met. He trusted her, though. He wanted to feel the same about Gavin, but he couldn't find that in himself.

"He still loves you as much as you do him. It'll take time, but the two of you will work through this."

"You sound so certain."

"Someone has to be." She smiled. "You'll get there; I don't doubt it for a second."

"Thanks." He wished he was this certain, but he'd use her assurance to bolster his own.

"In the meantime, do you have plans Friday night?"

"I'm going to guess I'm spending it with you."

"Perfect." She grinned. "Emily has a friend coming into town, and she asked me to show him around. She assures me he's charming and intelligent and handsome. You know this city better than I do so…"

"You want me to be the third wheel on your date?" That sounded less than fun. Jealousy nibbled his nerves.

Cyn studied him, brows furrowed. "It's not a date."

"Does he know that? Because your friend is trying to set you up."

"Emily wouldn't."

"You'd know better than me. I'm sure I'm reading too much into it." He was pretty sure he wasn't, but he was also relieved Cyn would rather have him there.

* * * *

Aaron locked up his moping. If he was going to spend the night on the town, even as a third wheel, he was going to enjoy it. Getting out would be good for him.

He spotted Cyn outside the restaurant as he approached. Her smile didn't reach her eyes, and her posture was stiff. The man she was talking to was handsome; Emily had been right about that. Light-brown hair, dark eyes, and the cut of his torso did dangerous things to his T-shirt.

If it were six months ago, he'd be the kind of guy Aaron went for. How fucked up was that? Now that he was technically single, he felt worse for looking than he ever had when he and Gavin were together.

Cyn's expression shifted to genuine as Aaron approached. "I'm glad you made it." She wrapped him in a hug, then stepped back. "This is Nathan. Nathan, Aaron."

"Great to meet you." Aaron shook his hand. Nathan's grip was firm, and his palm warm.

"Same." Nathan nodded at the Planet Hollywood. "Thanks, both of you, for indulging my tourist side. I bet both of you are sick of places like this."

"I've never been," Cyn said.

Aaron shook his head. "Same." Gavin would never go near here, with hordes of people all hoping to catch a glimpse of... whatever star-seekers were looking for.

"Awesome." Nathan draped an arm over each of them and steered them toward the entrance. "We'll be awkward tourists together. I've got a few friends who insist the last thing you do when you visit a new place is hit up the tourist spots, but I say that's like going to France and avoiding the Eiffel Tower or the Louvre."

Aaron laughed. "I don't know that anyone has ever compared Planet Hollywood to The Louvre."

"Which is one of the many reasons you'll enjoy my company this evening. Two seconds." Nathan left them to approach the host station.

Inside was a painful expansion of the neon and concrete that decorated the building front. The neon theme continued along booths and tables and display after display of memorabilia and people. There were many voices, Aaron could barely hear himself think. He didn't have to wallow. He couldn't ignore the outside world, which meant he was required to exist in it. It was exactly what he needed.

"If you bail early, I'll understand." Cyn's comment was soft, meant for Aaron's ears.

He glanced at her. Her grimace looked plastered on. He squeezed her fingers. "I'll be fine. We'll have fun."

She raised her brows. "Really?"

"Absolutely." If he thought about it, the answer would be *I don't know*, but here, he didn't have to think.

Nathan joined them again. "Lady and gentleman, our table awaits." He gave a deep bow and gestured toward a host waiting with menus.

They were seated at a table in the middle of the dining room, surrounded by people. It had been years since Gavin was willing to put up with something like this. Even when they visited busy places, he tipped his way into the quietest corner of the room.

"Are you two an item? Thing? Couple?" Nathan looked between Aaron and Cyn.

Aaron's *no* died in his throat, and he didn't know why.

"We're not." Cyn didn't seem to have any trouble spitting it out. Which was appropriate.

Aaron should follow up the response with a, *Because I'm in a long-term relationship*. That stuck in his throat too. He wasn't sure which was the bigger deception—keeping it to himself or saying it aloud.

"Excellent." Nathan leaned in, gaze lingering on Aaron. "Then I won't feel like an ass for hitting on you."

Which was Aaron's cue to mention Gavin.

Fuck that. They'd had an open relationship, and now that Gavin had ended things, Aaron was going to hesitate? No. If he was going to do tonight, he might as well try to enjoy it.

Cyn coughed.

Their waiter chose that moment to interrupt for their drink orders.

"Iced tea for me," Cyn said.

Nathan studied the cocktail page. "If you had to pick, would you go with the 'Hellboy' or the 'Iron Man'?"

There was no way those were drink names. Aaron flipped to the list, and sure enough, they also had a 'Gorillas in the Mist' and a 'Legally Blonde'. It was ridiculous. Who the hell took something like that seriously?

"I'm an 'Iron Man' kind of guy, personally," the waiter said.

"Perfect. Get me one of those."

"You know what?" Aaron shoved down the internal protest at what he was about to do. "Give me a 'Hellboy'. Might as well try them both." He couldn't remember the last time he had a drink, but if he was eating and only had the one, he should be able to handle the liquor fine. And it wasn't as if he was driving.

"Emily tells me you're an honest-to-God matchmaker." Nathan looked at Cyn. "And you have a way to filter out the creeps."

She shook her head. "*Creeps* is a subjective term. I get to pick my clientele."

"And the science starts after that?"

"Yup." Cyn managed to clip off the short word.

A memory flashed through Aaron's mind—the day she pitched her company in the VC offices, and what she told him after. Some people didn't work with her algorithm. Based on the tight line of Cyn's jaw, he had a feeling Nathan fell into that category.

Aaron didn't have a problem with that. He wasn't looking for an algorithm to tell him the guy was attractive and some of the most high-energy fun he'd seen in a long time.

Their drinks arrived, and Aaron let the first gulp burn down his throat. Getting drunk was only a mask. He wasn't interested in it being a long-term solution, but fuck if right now it didn't sound brilliant. Another bonus to the night.

Nathan cringed when he took a swallow of his. "Pineapple juice. Ugh. I need to learn to read." He looked more amused than annoyed and held out his glass. "Trade me?"

"Sure." Aaron swapped drinks with him.

"You work with Emily, right?" Cyn's tone was strained. "You're a programmer?"

"For her sister in law. Rather, I guess technically not by marriage, but Tara might as well be. And it's all the same company. But my contract there ended a week ago. You're on the matchmaking board of directors?" Nathan kept most of his attention focused on Aaron.

Cyn looked surprised at the question. Did she tell him that? Aaron didn't miss that Nathan avoided half of her question. He had a lot in common with

Gavin, including the rapid-fire dialog to keep the conversation going the way he wanted. There wasn't a dark cloud floating over Nathan's head, though.

"I've always wondered how that works. *Board member*. Is that a profession? Something you get hired for? What does your resume look like?"

It's complicated. Aaron bit back the answer. A statement like that bred curiosity, and he didn't want to linger on the topic. "You know how it goes. Independently wealthy because I cashed out of my first IPO at twenty-five, so I kick it and go where I feel like."

Nathan laughed. "I don't know if you're joking, though I have a feeling you're not. I love it either way."

Aaron finished his drink and ordered another with his meal. Fuck the outside world. There was too much potential for fun tonight.

CHAPTER TWENTY-TWO

A few hours later, the three of them sat in a rum bar Nathan had heard about online. The place was a dive, and as crowded as Planet Hollywood had been. Aaron loved it. Energy thrummed in the air, around the people and through him.

Or maybe that was the liquor and the fact that Nathan sat so his thigh brushed Aaron's. The pleasant buzz in Aaron's skull tried to insist that there was a red halo around Nathan's head. It was just the bar lights, but Aaron liked the contradicting visual.

Cynthia pushed back from the table. "I'm thinking of calling it a night."

Aaron grasped her fingers.

"Not yet. Soon," Nathan said.

"Why Italy?" Aaron brought the topic back to where it was before the interruption.

"I wanted a change of scenery." A goofy smile played on Nathan's face. "And it was a change. God, the things I've seen there. Not God, actually. Went to The Vatican and everything. His calendar was booked."

It was only a chuckle-worthy joke, but that

didn't stop Aaron from laughing. "I'd love to leave everything behind and go like that."

Cynthia frowned. "It's not for everyone."

"It worked for Emily. Hell, half the people in the office were from someplace else." Nathan's eyes were bright, and his suggestion light. "I know. You should come back with me when I fly out in a few days."

Cynthia tugged free of Aaron's grasp. Her mask was gone, replaced with a scowl that etched itself into all her features. If she was upset because of Gavin, or for whatever reason, she didn't have a right to be. Aaron didn't make that decision, and he was fucking tired of letting it devour him.

So when he said, "I can't," his words caught him off-guard.

"You sure?" Nathan leaned close enough his breath caressed Aaron's cheek. He smelled like tequila and aftershave, and it made Aaron's head swim. "*Independently wealthy*, right? You can occupy a board seat from another country."

"It's tempting…" Aaron wanted to say *yes*. Why couldn't he?

Nathan brushed his lips over Aaron's. There were no sparks, but fuck, if the blood didn't rush from Aaron's head and straight to his cock.

"Yup. I'm done. You two enjoy each other." Irritation dripped from Cyn's words.

"We will. Thanks for the hookup." Nathan waved at her.

Aaron shoved down the creeping guilt and hurt, cupped Nathan's face between his palms, and dove in for another kiss. A groan escaped Aaron's throat, and he pressed closer. They locked lips so long his thoughts swayed.

Or maybe that was the alcohol. Aaron didn't know or care. Time slowed to a crawl, as his tongue danced with Nathan's and their hands roamed everywhere, exploring.

It was such a simple thing—making out in the middle of a bar—but it made Aaron's pulse hammer in his ears and filled him with a giddiness he hadn't experienced in ages. They broke apart with twin gasps.

"Do you want to head back to my place? Take this somewhere more private?" Aaron asked. He ignored the doubt screaming in the back of his skull. The booze made that easier, which was pleasant.

"Fuck yes."

In the taxi, Aaron didn't keep his hands to himself. He dove back into the kissing, running his fingers along Nathan's chest, and falling into the sensation of Nathan's lips on his neck and ears.

They were a tangle of limbs as they rode the elevator up to the condo. Aaron was tempted to push him back against the wall, drop to his knees, and suck him off. The way Nathan's erection dug into him, it was clear the desire flowed both ways.

The seconds it took to stumble their way to the door were excruciating. Aaron unlocked it, and pushed Nathan inside.

As they stepped into the house, Gavin's familiar scent drilled into Aaron's thoughts, and his mind ground to a halt. He couldn't smell anything else. His stomach churned.

Nathan looked around the room, gaze

pausing on the pictures near the TV. "Are you… with someone?" For the first time that night, hesitation leaked into his voice.

"I was, but he's gone." Aaron pulled Nathan back to him. Desperation clawed inside, to find what they had seconds earlier.

Nathan studied him. "So I'm the rebound fuck?"

"Is that a problem?"

"Not at all." Nathan kissed him again, hard and hungrily, gripped Aaron's cock through his jeans and stroked.

Aaron groaned against his mouth, trying to slide back into the moment. Focus on the physical. Force out the thoughts. It didn't work. Aaron broke away with a sigh. "I'm sorry. I can't do this after all."

"I get it. No worries." Nathan's smile was back, but now it looked more like Cyn's had most of the night. He stepped around Aaron. "For what it's worth, he's a lucky guy, and he was stupid to give you up."

"Thanks." Aaron locked the door behind Nathan, then collapsed on the sofa. He didn't agree with Nathan's words. It wasn't a one-way street with Gavin. They were both lucky, and the fault flowed two ways as well.

Aaron's gut churned, and the pleasant buzz was gone. In its place, he found himself drowning in *shittiest boyfriend ever.*

* * * *

Cynthia sat next to Gavin on a bench in the

garden. "I can see why this is a perfect recovery spot. It's gorgeous here." She could almost forget the outside world existed. Until the same image flashed through her mind that had tormented her since it imprinted—Nathan kissing Aaron. She was furious on Gavin's behalf, and used that to convince herself there was no jealousy mingled in. She didn't give a shit who or what Aaron did, as it related to her.

"It is nice." Gavin looked relaxed. At peace. And more handsome than she remembered. "Are you all right?"

"I should be asking you that." She couldn't bring herself to tell him about last night. Didn't even know how to classify it. It wasn't technically cheating, was it?

"I'm great. Working through a lot of crap. I have baggage. Who knew?"

"I think most people do. You're just confronting yours." She'd lose herself in this conversation, and things would be fine. The shock of last night would wear off, and she'd realize she was overreacting.

"I suppose." His tone was easy and casual. "Why didn't you pursue psychology?"

She studied his expression. She didn't know what she was looking for.

"You told me you had a degree. I was curious—why get something that involved, and then not use it?"

She'd forgotten they talked about that. It warmed her from the inside that he remembered. "I use it. It's part of my business. But in the context you mean? I'm too cynical, and I have a horrible bedside manner."

"You're easy to talk to. Maybe not for other people, but for me, since that first day."

She didn't have to ask what he was talking about. The memory shifted the heat to scorch her skin and make her pulse race. "In my office? Where the two of you…"

"Almost talked you out of your panties."

"Not what I would have said." Because she couldn't find a more subtle way to put it.

"But you were thinking it."

"Guilty." She couldn't hide her amusement. "But I assumed that kind of conversation was status quo for you."

"Nah. Most people don't appreciate when Aaron and I do that. It tends to piss them off. But you fell into it."

A soft breeze carried through the garden, ruffling her hair and kissing away the flames in her cheeks and filling her nostrils with the sweet scent of flowers. It all mingled with Gavin's easy attitude and helped her relax. "It was fun. It always is with you two." *Was?*

"Which is my point. As far as I'm concerned, you're one of the best listeners in the world."

"Thanks." She wasn't sure what else to say to that.

He shifted in his seat so he was facing her. "What's your diagnosis?"

"Excuse me?" She turned as well. The scenery here was nice, but looking him in the eye was better.

"Despite what you said, that night at dinner,

you made an off-the-cuff diagnosis. I'm wondering if it's still the same, and what it is."

It was dangerous territory to step into, under the best circumstances. Unethical, potentially damaging, and a sure-fire way to ruin a friendship if she said the wrong thing. "I think you're intelligent and compassionate and trying to figure out where you fit in the world. You're looking everywhere and…" She bit the inside of her cheek. No need to say more.

"You're holding back."

"Do you blame me?"

He raised her head to meet his gaze. "I promise not to use what you say against you."

She wanted to shake her head in refusal, but didn't want to break the contact or lose the intensity of his gaze. She could fall into those eyes. "I still can't."

"I'll help." He cupped her neck and traced a thumb along the line of her jaw. "I'm looking everywhere for answers, and resenting myself and others when I can't find them or they're not what I want to hear."

She didn't like how close to home the words hit, not just for him, but her. Not that their circumstances were the same. She'd lived a vanilla suburban life, and the worst thing that had ever happened to her was when she pissed off her best friend. She still regretted the way she pushed Emily away, but that was nothing compared to what Gavin and Aaron were going through. She didn't think a phone call and a bit of groveling would repair their rift. "That's not the way I would have phrased it," she said.

"No, but it's what you were thinking. About me and about you."

"How do you do that?" she asked.

"Hmm?"

"Reach in my head and pluck out my thoughts."

He tucked a strand of hair behind her ear. "I don't. I can only tell you what's on *my* mind." He dipped his head, and her breath caught.

When he kissed her, softly and sweetly, her thoughts evaporated. She leaned into him and rested her palms against his chest. He slid his hand to the back of her neck, holding her tight and deepening the kiss.

She gripped his shirt, needing to hold onto something to stay grounded. The outdoor scents mingled with his aftershave. Need unfurled inside, flowing through her veins. This wasn't right, but it felt that way. Conflict trickled inside, and she tried to bottle it.

He pushed up the bottom of her shirt. His palm scorched her already hot skin. She wanted to keep going. Sink into his touch and attention.

Logic revolted inside, and she summoned more strength than she thought she had, to push him back. "Aaron," she forced out. It was a stupid thing to say, especially given what she witnessed last night. Why couldn't she enjoy this? Because it wasn't right. Because Gavin and Aaron belonged together, and it was obvious they still loved each other, regardless of everything either of them had done.

Gavin's pout was laced with a playful glint.

"We broke up."

She hated and adored that he made that look good. "Bullshit, you did."

"Fine. You're right." He slumped back, breaking all contact. "But what if the temporary becomes permanent? I fucked up pretty hard. He'd be justified in not waiting for me."

He's not. She swallowed the retort. She didn't know what transpired after she left. Probably exactly what she assumed, but she couldn't blurt out things that she didn't have proof of. "If that's what happens, then so be it, but you can't give up. You belong together." As she said the words, something new pinged inside. A confession she hadn't let herself vocalize until now. It was going to hurt like hell to be on the outside of their relationship after all this, but she couldn't be selfish with something as solid and real as what she saw between them.

"Besides"—anger surged inside, raw and unexpected—"you don't get to do this to me. Use me as a replacement, to fill the hole in your heart."

"I'm not—"

"Don't." If she let him speak, he'd talk her out of what she was feeling. "You might not think that's what you're doing, but this doesn't go anywhere. Whether you leave Aaron or you and he get back together, you and I don't have that kind of relationship. If my friendship means so little to you that you're willing to fuck it away, to replace the emptiness inside? I don't want to be a part of that."

"Cynthia, that's not what this is." He grabbed her wrist as she stood.

"Then what is it?" She looked him in the eye,

refusing to read anything into the pleading in his expression. "Explain it."

"I can't."

She jerked out of his grasp. "Then I'm done here." Walking away hurt more than she expected, but not as much as suspecting he would have been happy to use her if she hadn't called him on it.

CHAPTER TWENTY-THREE

In his skull, Gavin shouted until he was hoarse. He kicked the wall, threw things across the room, and stomped his feet like a toddler at his worst tantrum. How dare Cynthia throw this back in his face? He wasn't doing any of the things she accused him of. If she wasn't interested, she could say so, instead of wrapping it in excuses.

Outside his head, he sat in the garden, staring at the ground, fingers knotted in his hair and forehead resting on his palms.

He'd been a first-class asshole. As much as he wanted to be furious with her, he was the one who didn't have his head on straight. He was everything Aaron had accused him of—selfish, irresponsible, and looking for a way to shift the blame to anybody who wasn't him.

He sat there as the sun drifted lower toward the horizon, until the sky flared with an orange-gray glow. It must be almost eight. Another thing he didn't like about all this thinking he'd been doing— time slipped away from him.

"Do you mind some company?" A female voice dragged him from his thoughts.

He looked up to see Dr. Sandy Hyde, his onsite therapist, settling onto the bench next to him. He wasn't in the mood to talk, but at the same time, being stuck in his thoughts wasn't helping any. He shrugged.

"You've been out here for a while." Her tone was conversational.

"It's pleasant out here. Quiet." He hadn't been in the mood to talk to her much since he arrived. Their first few sessions consisted of him trying to push back on her, to figure out what made her tick. The woman was a fucking brick wall, though, so he'd dialed himself back to one-word answers. He didn't want anyone poking around in his head if he couldn't do the same in return. It wasn't a fair trade.

"It is."

Gavin waited for her to say something else. Seconds ticked away. He glanced at her, and she gave him a smile before returning her attention to the garden. He knew how this worked. She hoped he'd talk to fill the void if she stayed silent. "Should we do this in your office?" he asked.

"Not my first choice for where I'd spend my Saturday night, but you're welcome to head in there if you'd like. I think I'll stay here."

He didn't want to dance around thoughts or feelings. He'd rather be wallowing in his frustration with life. The sooner she left, the sooner he could do that. "This isn't going to work."

"What's not?"

Gavin clenched his jaw. "Whatever you're doing. I don't want to talk. I'm not going to spill my guts just because you joined me." Had he said too much? That implied there was something for him to spill.

She studied his face for a moment, her expression as blank and impossible to read as always, except for the pity in her eyes. "What I'm doing is enjoying the evening. Anything you read into it beyond that is you projecting."

"Which is your goal." This was the most he'd gotten her to say since he arrived. If he poked a little more, could he find his angle with the doctor?

"If you say so."

Gavin's irritation surged until it spilled out in a growl, and he stood. "I'm done here. Enjoy your evening, Dr. Hyde." His feet didn't move him toward the building, though.

"All right. I'll tell you what I'm thinking," she said. "There's never a single solution to any problem in life. Different things work for different people. However, there's frequently an answer that works for most people. Some will sneer and say, *That's stupid. It'll never work.* Others will swear they want to do things that way, but never get around to it. Only a very small number of people will try it before deciding whether or not it's for them."

Gavin had a suspicion about where this was going, but he kept his mouth shut. No reason to give her the satisfaction.

She raised her brows. "Doesn't matter the problem. It always works that way. This place—it's a rehabilitation clinic. People are here because someone wanted them to find a solution. It was either their decision or a loved one's. You checked yourself in. If you wanted to dry out and move on with life, you picked an expensive way to do it."

"But I'm not any of those. I don't have a problem with the solution or giving it my all, but I don't like soul-baring to be a one-way street." *Fuck.* He didn't mean to say that.

"That's how therapy works. I'm not your friend; I'm a mirror. The high-quality, makeup kind that shows off every pore and detail. If I reflect myself back at you, it doesn't do you any good."

He didn't like the analogy. Or maybe it was the little Aaron voice inside, saying *she's got a point*, that Gavin didn't care for. "That's not going to work for me."

"Because you're used to people bending to your will. To poking and prodding until you get the answer you want."

Anger amplified his irritation. She didn't have the right to make a snap analysis of him. That was one of the things he wanted to avoid. He wasn't going to show she'd gotten under his skin, though. Saying, *So do you,* felt like an articulate version of, *It takes one to know one.* He'd go for the rational response instead. "If that were the case, I wouldn't be hounded by fans. My boyfriend would understand where I was coming from. Cynthia wouldn't have walked out of here upset."

Way to keep blaming everyone else. This time, the voice was his. When he was a child, people fell over themselves to give him what he wanted. If someone didn't comply, they didn't understand or were stupid or had cut their Hollywood career short.

But Gavin outgrew that kind of selfishness. As an adult, he knew the world didn't revolve around him.

Dr. Hyde never flinched. "Are you here to address what's really going on, or just get sober long enough to put yourself back in your loved ones' lives?"

"I'm going to bed." Gavin headed toward the door. Fucking psychological games and bullshit.

Retreat didn't help. Perhaps because he didn't get the final word, despite speaking last. He spent the night struggling to get comfortable, and failing. By about three in the morning, he gave up and lay on his back.

His Sunday was a lot the same, but by Monday morning he had the solution. Go back to the way things were. Walk into Dr. Hyde's office for his appointment, present the same brick wall she showed him, and prove he could be a mirror too.

He took the same seat he always did, skipping the couch and opting for the chair across from her.

She gave him a warm smile. "I wondered if you'd be here today."

Which was close to what he expected she'd say. He had his first few lines rehearsed and he'd improv from there. *Of course I'm here*, he'd tell her in a pleasant tone. *I want to get better.*

"This is fucking bullshit." No, no, *no*. That wasn't what was supposed to come out. He could still backtrack. "You've got the nerve to tell me *I* don't want to get better? To call me manipulative? That's what you do for a fucking living—turn people's words back on them."

"I didn't say any of those things."

"But that's what you meant."

"Did I?"

"Just *fucking stop*." Gavin ground his teeth when the words came out as a shout. "You don't know anything about my situation beyond what's on the admissions forms and gossip blogs. You don't have anywhere near enough information to make assumptions or—God forbid—a bullshit diagnosis."

"You're right; I don't. Prove me wrong."

He gave a dark chuckle. "Fine. But not because you tricked me into it."

"I'm not trying to trick you into anything. Mirror, remember? But if you'd like a more direct question, who's Cynthia?"

Intelligent. Attractive. Infuriating. Sexy. But none of those words answered the *who* question. He wasn't about to say *I don't know*, and he wasn't interested in digging deeper. The idea he'd treated Cynthia wrong gnawed at his joints until he ached. "She owns a company my partner invested in." That was a simple truth. Deceptive, but simple.

"The partner you severed ties with? Aaron?"

"I've only ever had the one." Another deceptively simple fact.

"Is he abusive?"

Gavin shook his head. "God no. He's incredible." At least that was true to its core.

Dr. Hyde crossed her legs at the knee. "I want you to think about this before you answer, because I'm not saying it's the case with the two of you. Abuse can come in a lot of forms. It doesn't have to be physical or intentional. Just as often, it's more of a feeling that he's taken control from you. That if you make the wrong decision, you'll be made to suffer."

The words hurt. "I accused him of that." The things Gavin had said slammed back into his thoughts like a freight train, knocking his brain offline.

"But it's not true?" Dr. Hyde's impassive mask was back.

"I didn't mean it. I shouldn't have said it."

"I see."

Gavin should be frustrated she returned to the basic responses, but he was starting to understand. It felt good to talk like this. Frightening, but also a relief. He needed to make this right. Even if Aaron didn't forgive him—though Gavin prayed to God he would—Gavin owed him a sincere apology. Admitting that to himself hurt, because it meant there was no one to blame but him. No wonder so many addicts stalled on Step Four. He was glad *steps* weren't part of the process here.

"Are you interested in having Aaron here, for some of these conversations?" Dr. Hyde asked.

The question caught Gavin off-guard. Or maybe it was that he didn't have an immediate response. "I don't know if he'd agree to something like that."

"Is he as stubborn as you?"

Gavin chuckled. "At least. But that's not why. Once upon a time, he'd have done anything to help me get better, but I really fucked up."

"You never know if he'll say *yes* until you ask."

* * * *

Gavin rambled through the hall, mind whirring with next steps to take. After leaving a note with the administration office, to update Aaron's status on his visitor list, it was time to make some calls.

Aaron didn't answer, and as disappointed as Gavin was, he wasn't surprised. There was no reason for cryptic notes or generic call-me messages. He needed to lay things on the line. When the voicemail beeped, he said, "It's me. I'm sorry. For so much more than I can sum up in the next minute, but it's a long list. I want a chance to prove it to you. To make things right. I'd like to see you, and if you're interested, introduce you to my therapist."

Cynthia didn't pick up either. Gavin was less certain of what to say to her, so he disconnected without leaving a message.

With Aaron, it was straightforward—Gavin loved and adored him, and owed him so much. When it came to Cynthia, Gavin had no idea where they stood or what they were. She took his calls as a friend. The sex was fun—incredible even. But if she were anyone else, he would have walked away without a second thought.

She wasn't *anyone else,* though. Besides Aaron, she was the only other person he really trusted. Really cared about. And he didn't know how to reconcile that with their lack of a relationship.

CHAPTER TWENTY-FOUR

Aaron stood on the balcony, staring out over the city but not registering it. He was trying his hardest to keep his mind blank. To shove aside thoughts about Gavin and Cyn, about the colossal fail the weekend was, about his lack of direction, and find his center.

A shrill chirp filtered through glass and shattered what little focus he had. *Phone.* He should ignore it and get back to his pseudo-meditation.

What if it's Gavin?

It wouldn't be. That didn't stop him from sprinting into the house, to find the ringing device. He grabbed it as it stopped ringing. Gavin's name sat on the screen above *Missed Call.*

Aaron's heart did a backflip that stuttered and fell flat. He forced the elation down. No celebrating until things were resolved, one way or the other. The *Voicemail* icon popped up next to the *Missed Call* image. He pulled up the message, fingers shaking with each swipe of the screen.

As he listened to Gavin's voice, the words, and the apology, a tentative smile flitted in. Aaron was done hesitating or wondering what next. He wasn't willing to let Gavin walk all over him, and he refused to put up with another round of, *I promise, never again,* followed by *once again.* But the rehab was new, and Gavin's idea. Aaron wasn't ready to give up on the relationship, and after the night with Nathan, he couldn't deny that he wanted Gavin in his life.

So he called him.

"Hey, honey. How's home?" Gavin's playful answer was cut with hesitation.

A fist squeezed around Aaron's lungs at the familiar voice and greeting. "Empty."

"I miss you."

Aaron swallowed past a lump in his throat. This wasn't the kind of thing that could be done over the phone, but comfort flowed through him. "Me too. But I haven't forgiven you."

"That's fair."

"It is?"

Gavin's laugh was dry. "I deserve it. I don't like it, but I figure this isn't the kind of thing that goes away with a simple apology."

"Or even a complex one." Even in a conversation like this, laced with tension and uncertainty, it was easy to fall into the back and forth. Aaron was grateful for that. "You said something about a visit?"

"I did. I'm hoping you'll come see me, and"—Gavin let out a shaky breath—"my therapist wants to meet you."

"Is that like meeting your folks, but without the—" Aaron snapped his jaw shut. Too tender a topic to delve into right now.

"Without the screaming and disowning? Not nearly so bad or stressful."

"I'd like that."

"Yeah?" Gavin's smile was almost visible over the line. "Pick a morning, any day this week, and be here at eleven."

"Tomorrow?"

"Perfect. I'll see you then. And I love you."

"I love you, too." Aaron felt a rush of relief. Finally, something felt right. Not fixed, but better than it had been in ages.

* * * *

Cynthia stared at the missed calls from Aaron and Gavin. If she was the friend she claimed to be, she'd call them both back and listen to what they had to say. Was she lying to herself, believing a connection existed?

It would take her a little while to come to terms with what happened with Gavin. Since Saturday, her fury had faded to hurt and then indignation. She didn't deserve to be treated like that.

But as annoyed as she was by the way Aaron shut her out, he hadn't technically done anything wrong. Except maybe lead Nathan on, and she prayed that wasn't the case.

She'd call Aaron back first. He was more likely to be up this time on a Sunday, anyway. Her phone rang in her hand, startling her, and an international number flashed on the screen. *Emily.* Based on how Cynthia left things with Aaron and Nathan, she wasn't sure she wanted to take the call, but she did want a friendly ear. "Hello?"

"*Ciao, bella.*" The words rolled off Emily's tongue.

Cynthia smiled. "Nice accent. Not that I'd know, but it sounds authentic to my uncultured ear."

"I've got a good teacher." The cheer in Emily's voice was contagious. "You busy?"

"Not really. I'm kind of a boring homebody when I'm not working. Same as always."

"Boring? Never. Especially not according to Nathan. He says he had a blast, and he's sorry he didn't get to tell you *goodbye* before he left."

Cynthia's gut sank at the name. "It's not a big deal. I'm glad he had fun." She tried to put some enthusiasm into her tone but failed.

"Are you okay?"

"Yeah. I'm just…" Cynthia sighed. Once upon a time, she would have told Emily everything that was going on, no hesitation. Now, it didn't feel right. Their friendship still felt tentative—As though Cynthia needed to re-earn the right to unburden herself.

"I'm listening, if you want to talk about it," Emily said sympathetically.

"I don't feel like I deserve that."

"So you fucked up. You realized your mistake, you apologized, and we're good."

Defensiveness rolled through Cynthia at all the blame falling on her, but it was appropriate. Still— "This is different. The one thing I don't think we're good on yet. I kind of…" She bit the inside of her cheek.

"You know you're killing me, don't you? If

you drag this out any longer, it won't matter what you say; it will be anti-climactic."

That would be a relief. Cynthia didn't like bottling all this. "After you left and I kicked Paul out, I didn't have anything to focus on but work. I pitched my way through all the VCs in Silicon Valley, and no one nibbled, so I moved to L.A. I told myself the clientele would be better here. More money. More focus on relationships and less on startups."

"Makes sense."

"But I hit more brick walls. Like an unfortunate crash-test dummy. Even with the last firm I was in, everyone in the room told me *no* except one guy. Investor number twenty-three." It was odd to think of Aaron in those terms. He was so much more.

"Sounds like a lucky number to me."

Cynthia's bitter laugh slipped out. "You'd think. He told me if I proved my product worked, he'd fund me."

"So… what was the catch?"

"Matching him and his boyfriend with a third person."

"Ah." Emily's tone was impossible to interpret. "Where did things go wrong?"

Cynthia was surprised Emily didn't assume the request itself was the start of the downhill slide. In a way, it was. "The system matched me. First time around, only me. They found out. I let things go too far." That was the bit she hated saying out loud. Especially to Emily.

"You fucked your investor."

Cynthia winced at the flat statement. "And

his boyfriend."

"After the shit you gave me."

"I told you this wasn't the kind of story you wanted to hear." Cynthia should have trusted her instinct and kept this to herself. She sank back onto her couch. It didn't have any answers, but it didn't judge, either.

"If I were vindictive, I'd love this story." Emily's tone softened. "I'm not. It's screwing with your head pretty bad?"

"Exactly. They're dysfunctional. I got attached…" Cynthia wanted to add more, but that summed it up nicely.

"*You* did? You're the queen of not getting attached."

It was true. Cynthia'd had more than her share of one-night stands and bar hookups, and none of them chipped her surface. Why did this one get under her skin? "I did this time. I swore to myself I was fine—"

"But sometimes you can't help it."

"Exactly." The topic sucked, but it was nice to talk to Emily like this again. Cynthia missed this closeness.

"If I were there, I'd bring you ice cream and wine," Emily said.

Cynthia smiled, and righted herself. "It's not the same, being alone."

"I wouldn't think so. It sounds kind of pathetic," Emily teased.

Cynthia laughed. "Thanks," she said sarcastically. She might not spend the night wallowing, but she would treat herself. She wandered into the kitchen and grabbed the ice cream from the freezer. She snagged a spoon and pushed herself onto the counter, the ice cream next to her and the phone balanced between her shoulder and ear.

"It can work, you know," Emily said.

"What can?"

"All three of you."

Cynthia stopped with the spoon halfway to her mouth. The possibility surged inside with hope, and she squashed it. That was about the worst place her mind could go. That path was littered with desire and want, and her heart in shattered fragments. Or she was being a tad melodramatic. "You don't know that."

"I'll admit it's not for everyone, but I do know it can work. Did Nathan tell you how he and I know each other?"

Curiosity swelling, Cynthia pushed her ice cream aside and searched her brain for what he'd said. "Something about being friends with your sister-in-law, but that she wasn't really but might as well have been. Does he always talk that fast?"

"Only on his best days. I won't make you jump through hoops for this. I'm in a relationship— a wonderful and amazing one—with two guys who love each other as much as they do me, and me them. It can work."

Cynthia's mind tilted off balance, making her dizzy, as she tried to process the news. "What? You don't just dump information like that on someone. You're... Really?"

"Take your time."

"I'm glad it's working for you." Cynthia

wasn't going to knock the relationship. Six months ago, she thought *happily ever after* was fairytale bullshit. When she met Gavin and Aaron, she started to adjust her way of thinking. Watching them fall apart hurt more than was logical.

If Emily was happy with two guys, more power to her. That didn't mean Cynthia could afford to give any attention to the hope growing inside. "These two are so dysfunctional," Cynthia said, "and broken and… they're so good together when they're not. I can't be a part of that."

"Do what's best for you. For real." Emily was kind. "If this is breaking your heart—and I can hear in your voice that it is—and you don't think they're good for you, walk away. But don't write them off because it's non-traditional."

"That wouldn't be in my top five reasons." Though the whole *dysfunctional* thing would rank near the top. Getting all of that out there, as much as the memories ached, lifted a weight from Cynthia's chest. "Thank you."

"I didn't do much."

"You listened. It's more than I deserve."

"Stop beating yourself up." A sharp edge lined Emily's words. "You learned. From what happened between you and me, and from what's going on now. You don't deserve to be shit on because you made a mistake."

The words sank deep into Cynthia's bones, triggering something she wasn't willing to acknowledge yet. Doing so would mean surrendering her anger at Gavin, and she wasn't ready.

CHAPTER TWENTY-FIVE

Aaron approached the front desk in the rehab clinic, and a sliver of smugness whispered through him. The guy working the counter was the same person who'd been there last time Aaron visited, trying to talk to Gavin.

The flash of recognition when the employee looked up said he probably remembered. "May I help you?"

"Aaron Birch. I'm here to see Gavin Jackson."

"Of course." The guy still never checked his computer. "Come right back. He's waiting."

Aaron swallowed the *damn straight* that wanted to be heard. "Thank you."

They traveled down a long hallway, and Aaron was pointed toward a room with an open door. Beyond recognizing it was an office, he didn't care about anything in the room except Gavin.

Aaron closed the distance between them in a few short strides, rested his palms on Gavin's face, and kissed him.

When Gavin pressed into him and kissed back, a weight lifted from Aaron that had settled in so long ago, he'd forgotten it was there.

A soft cough interrupted the moment, and Aaron broke away with a gasp.

A woman sat a few feet away, watching them, a half-smile threatening to crack her otherwise blank face.

Gavin laughed—God, Aaron missed that sound—and nodded at her. "Aaron, this is my shrink, Dr. Sandy Hyde. Dr. Hyde, this is the love of my life."

She rose and extended her hand. "Pleasure to meet you."

"Same." Aaron shook her hand, then looked back at Gavin. "I'm sure she's a wonderful doctor, but can we catch up without an audience?"

"I'm not here to judge; I'm only a facilitator." Dr. Hyde said.

"Is *facilitating* code for feeding Gavin his lines?" Aaron winced as the passive-aggressive question passed his lips. "I apologize."

"Are you sorry?" she asked.

"Of course I am." Aaron stared at her, as Gavin tugged him to sit.

"Then why did you say it?"

"It slipped out." Aaron didn't like being put on the defensive, especially at the start of a conversation. Gavin put up with this? "Sometimes that happens. I'm not the one who's here to be psychoanalyzed, but I am owed an apology."

"All right." She nodded.

"What's that supposed to mean?" Aaron's elation at seeing Gavin again faded behind the odd confrontation. He was overreacting and letting himself be baited, but it was weeks since he talked to Gavin, and now they had to go through a translator? "No, wait. Don't ask me what I think it means."

"I wasn't planning on it. What would you like an apology for?"

"Gavin knows."

"But I'd like to hear your version," Dr. Hyde said.

"It's okay," Gavin squeezed Aaron's hand. "Aaron's right. I owe him an apology. For blaming my problems on him. For not listening. For running away instead of facing reality. For turning to someone else for comfort when I had an incredible man by my side."

Guilt and the name *Nathan* wormed their way through Aaron's thoughts. It didn't matter how hard he tried to convince himself that night was okay, since nothing happened, the regret still gnawed at his senses. He forced the thoughts aside and clung to indignation. "See?"

"This is where you say, *It's all right; I forgive you,*" Gavin teased.

"Except that's what I've always done, and if it were all right, we wouldn't be here."

Gavin's smile slipped. "I know. I don't expect it to be that easy, but I'm willing to make the effort to get us there."

That was the first time Aaron had heard Gavin phrase it that way. In the past it was always, *It'll never happen again. I promise*, but there was no substance to the words. Nothing to back them up. Maybe the new language was thanks to Dr. Hyde, but Gavin sounded sincere. He believed what he was saying, which made Aaron do the same.

"Me too." Aaron looked at the doctor. "What happens next?"

"What do you want to happen next?" she asked.

Aaron twisted his mouth in frustration. "That's not helpful."

"It's more useful than you think." Gavin chuckled. "And she does a lot of it. I'm not done in here. I need more time to sort through things, but my hope is you'll stick with me while I do."

Aaron's reassurance died in his throat as he remembered Nathan again. Could he make a promise like that given what he'd already done?

Gavin's laugh was more nervous this time. "That's not a good sign."

"I'm here for you." Aaron meant that. "If you're trying, I'll stick by your side."

"But?"

"You're not the only one at fault." If they were owning up to things, Aaron needed to take responsibility too. "I've made my share of bad decisions. Taking a job I hated, and then resenting you for not making the same mistake. Thinking the best way to fix *us* was to keep our relationship open. Friday night…"

Gavin furrowed his brow. "What happened Friday night?"

"I got drunk. I brought a guy home and almost fucked him… It doesn't sound that bad out loud, but up until we walked in the door, I wanted him to stay."

Gavin's expression relaxed. "But you didn't do anything. I made a play for your business partner and pissed her off."

Cynthia. Jealousy surged in. Aaron didn't have a right to feel that, though. Not about her.

"My bad, number five-hundred and ninety-three." Gavin shrugged. "I'll apologize to her if she'll let me, but she's not the kind of person who will let that impact her working relationship with you."

That hadn't been Aaron's first concern, though it should be. "Thanks. So I guess we're both willing to work on this?"

Gavin nodded.

"Are you willing to join Gavin for therapy once or twice a week?" Dr. Hyde asked.

"Yes," Aaron said. He'd put up with a mediator for a few hours a week, if it meant he and Gavin got their life back.

Schedules were set, and Dr. Hyde called the session to a close, so she could meet with her next appointment.

Aaron tangled his fingers with Gavin's as they left. "Do I get the grand tour?" he asked.

"Absolutely." Gavin led him through the halls.

The place could have been any mid-range hotel. Even the guests reminded Aaron of weary business travelers, trudging through their day and trying not to let life crush them.

Except here, there was an underlying thread of hope that getting out from under that weight was possible. The thought almost made him smile.

They stopped in front of a door, and Gavin opened it. He gestured inside. "We'll start with my humble dwellings."

From the full-size bed to the polished-but-generic dresser, a TV on top, the room matched the rest of the place—it would fit in any generic motel.

Gavin tugged him inside, kicked the door shut, and—palms to Aaron's—pinned his hands to the wall on either side of his head. Gavin dragged his mouth along Aaron's jaw and down his neck, alternating between sucking and licking. Being pressed so close, Gavin's heat surrounding him, and that familiar scent made Aaron instantly hard.

"I've been thinking…" Gavin said between kisses.

"About how much you missed this? Because that's all I'm thinking about right now."

Gavin pulled back long enough to give him a smirk, before yanking Aaron's shirt over his head. "Definitely missed this. Which led to the next thought."

"I'd make another guess, but if you get to the point, we can lose the rest of our clothes, right?" Aaron didn't have the mental capacity for conversation when Gavin was nipping along his chest.

"Exactly." Gavin paused, straightened, and met his gaze. "Give me your attention for thirty seconds, then fucking."

"Thirty. Twenty-nine. Twenty-eight."

Gavin rolled his eyes but kept smiling. "I've been thinking that, as fun as it is to sometimes share a third person, and while the idea of an open relationship sounds all carefree, I want you to myself for a while. I'm not ruling anything out in the future, but—"

"I agree. Just you and me." *What about Cyn?* Aaron silenced the thought before it could take root. This was perfect. Aaron kissed him, diving his tongue into Gavin's mouth and pressing close for all he was worth. The way his heart soared and excitement sparked over his skin at Gavin's touch was addictive. Aaron felt the same electricity now as when they were seventeen and exploring this for the first time.

Aaron dragged his fingers along Gavin's chest, tracing the familiar and enticing lines of definition on his way down. He reached the bottom and yanked Gavin's shirt off. The feeling of bare skin on bare skin sent desire racing over him. He fell back into the kiss. Flattened between Gavin and the door, he couldn't think of any place he'd rather be.

He dropped his hand and stroked Gavin's erection through his jeans.

Gavin bucked against his touch, then leaned into him with a groan. "I can do better than that." Gavin's hot breath fell across Aaron's cheek.

"It's not a contest." Aaron's laugh faded into a groan when Gavin kissed down his chest, unbuckling Aaron's belt at the same time.

Gavin knelt and unzipped Aaron's jeans, teasing his cock through the boxer briefs. Aaron groaned at the light scrape of teeth over fabric. Gavin freed him, and when he wrapped his hot palm around Aaron's shaft, Aaron jerked against his hand.

Gavin stroked Aaron's cock, slowly at first and building to an intense pace. Voices traveled through the door as people passed the room, and though no one was going to burst in without knocking, Aaron felt like they were getting away with something wicked. He bucked his hips in time with Gavin's pumping, and his breath came in short bursts.

The sensation pulled him in, but didn't push him to climax. He hovered near climax, head swimming and stars dancing at the edge of his vision.

Gavin took him in his mouth, and Aaron almost came when he hit the back of Gavin's throat. He knotted his fingers in Gavin's hair, needing something to hold onto.

His legs wobbled, and his thoughts fluttered away. The only thing in his head was the array of touches racing over him—Gavin's tongue on his hyper sensitive skin, while he caressed his sac.

As orgasm built inside, then burst forward, every muscle in Aaron's body tensed before he relaxed. He spurted in Gavin's mouth, hips grinding until he was spent.

Gavin slowed. With each gentle suck, a fresh shudder of pleasure coursed through Aaron, until his cock slid free, cool air hitting it.

He sank to the floor as his legs refused to support him any longer. With a shaky laugh, he kissed Gavin. He dove into the moment, tasting himself on Gavin's lips. They sat there for a moment, until Aaron caught his breath. Then he teased Gavin's erection through his slacks. "What do you want?"

Gavin shook his head, slid to sit next to Aaron, and pulled him into his arms. "Just this," he said. "This is all about you, and right now, you're the only thing I want."

Aaron didn't have an argument for that.

CHAPTER TWENTY-SIX

Cynthia sifted resumes into folders in her email—*absolutely not, looking good*, and *meh*. If there was one task she hadn't accounted for, time-wise, this was it. It would be easier once she'd filled most of her open positions, but for now, it ate into her schedule. She foresaw another long night in the office.

Fine with her. Staying here to work kept her on task. Earlier in the week, she'd eliminated the excuse of house calls to Aaron, telling him over email that due to time constraints, she'd only be able to see him at her office, with an appointment, during business hours.

It hurt to send the email. It ached almost as much to see his terse reply—*I understand*—but she'd brought any wounded feelings on herself.

She turned her attention to the next applicant, and relief whispered through her when she saw the *pending* folder was empty. Now there was a new issue. She had potential candidates for all of her open positions, except development—the one place she was pickiest about, and the one she needed the most help with. Emily did a lot of the work when they were building the application; Cynthia wouldn't be able to run the company and maintain so much code.

Her desk phone rang, and *Reception* flashed on the screen. She hit the *Speaker* button. "Yes?"

"Your two o'clock is here," the pleasant female voice said.

Aaron. "Thanks. Send him back." Cynthia tried to swallow the surge of anxiety that pulsed through her. She hadn't seen him since the night they went out with Nathan, and had managed to avoid any conversation with him beyond business. The in-person meeting would require a balance of politeness and professionalism she didn't know if she could manage.

"Afternoon." His greeting drew her attention. He looked better than he had in weeks. No more shadows under his eyes. A smile tugged up his mouth. And he still looked as drop-dead irresistible in a suit as the night they met.

"Hey." She pasted on a smile and stood to shake his hand. A pulse of familiarity raced through her at his firm grip, and she swallowed. "Have a seat."

When he took the chair across from her, memories tumbled loose, of he and Gavin sitting there, answering questions and making her squirm in the best way possible. Was it hot in here? She needed to check the thermostat when she was done with the meeting. "Thanks for coming down. It's easier for me than breaking away, with travel time and all."

"No problem."

She didn't like the stilted conversation, but it would get easier. "How are you doing?" It would be rude not to ask. And if he gave her a generic *fine*, it would silence the part of her that would rather sit and chat and make sure he was all right, than focus on business.

"Good. Really good." His smile grew.

She couldn't help herself. She wanted to know. *Don't pretend it's anything other than polite, and you'll be fine.* "Oh?"

"I talked to Gavin—saw him—a few days ago. We're fixing things."

Cynthia almost choked on the bittersweet combination of joy for them and something darker on her part. "That's fantastic." She meant it. "I told you the two of you were fated."

"You held a stronger hope than I did."

"That's bullshit. You knew. You weren't ready to give up. I'm glad the two of you pulled your heads out of your asses." She teased. No. Wrong direction to go in. "So should we get down to business?"

"Cyn, we don't have to dial things back this far. We're still friends."

The words gouged at her heart. "It's *Cynthia*, and we do need to draw this line. We can't keep it blurry or vague or as *just a suggestion*. If we do that, in the long run someone gets hurt, and the business falls apart, and if we establish boundaries, that won't be an issue."

"You got it." The friendliness faded from his eyes, replaced with a sadness she wished she could ignore.

Her stance felt harsh, but after the last time she saw Gavin, she needed to do away with any assumptions. Otherwise it would hurt too much when it was over. Being part of Aaron and Gavin's world was fun while it lasted, but Cynthia wasn't a permanent fixture in their romance, and this was the best way to keep that in mind.

* * * *

It was good to be home. Gavin didn't mind the accommodations at the clinic, but after four weeks, he was happy to be out. He stepped into the condo and stalled in the doorway, letting familiarity wash over him.

Aaron tossed Gavin's bags aside—he'd managed to come home with a lot, for someone who went away with only the clothes on his back—and kissed him on the back of the neck before stepping around him.

The sound of the door closing filled the room. Aaron grabbed Gavin's hand and tugged him to the couch. He sat and prompted him to do the same. "Put your things away later. I want to enjoy this for a bit," Aaron said. He leaned his back against Gavin's chest.

"I'm great with that." Gavin draped his arms over Aaron's shoulders. A comfortable silence settled between them. The last couple of weeks had helped Gavin dig into his head more than he ever would have admitted was necessary. Some days it was okay, and others it hurt worse than any physical wound. He went through therapy almost every day, though, only taking weekends off. Aaron's visits were a lot of the same.

Sitting here, not saying anything, was its own

kind of soothing.

Gavin had only seen Cynthia the once, while he was there. Her name bounded into his skull without permission and jarred his calm. She called him back a few days after he spoke with Aaron for the first time. Gavin tried to apologize, and she insisted he didn't need to. She said they needed clearer boundaries, and she was setting those. Told him they had a lot of fun, but Aaron was her investor, Gavin was Aaron's partner, and anything else was behind them.

The memory gnawed at his senses, chipping away at the joy of being back where he belonged. He shouldered it aside and shifted to rest his cheek against Aaron's.

"What do you want to be when you grow up?" Gavin asked, keeping the teasing in his voice. He was tired of talking and thinking about himself.

Aaron gave a light laugh. "Not a clue. Independently wealthy? The way we invested, we're set for a long time, as long as we're not careless."

"Sounds boring."

"It is. A month unemployed, and I don't know what to do with myself."

Gavin dug through surface thoughts. "Day trading? Or you could get a weekend job in Tahoe, dealing cards. *Counting* cards."

"I'm done with the shell games, large scale or small," Aaron said. "And I'll drive you nuts if I'm around the house all the time, not working."

"I won't notice while I'm working. But it won't bother me either way."

Aaron glanced back, brows raised. "What are

you going to do?"

This answer was simple—the one thing he enjoyed on an almost Zen level. "Get back into development. High end. Complicated."

"Just like that?"

"Not *just*. It's been a few years; I need to touch up my skills. But I miss it. *Oh*." Inspiration struck. "I know what you should do."

"Professional yacht racing?"

Gavin stared at the back of Aaron's head, puzzled. "First of all, where the fuck did that come from? Second, you hate sailing."

Aaron shifted on the couch to look at him. "This would be racing. Entirely different from sailing. Besides, when I did the whole venture-capitalist thing, I thought it would be the best job ever, to help people realize their dreams, and look at how that turned out. I figured I'd pick something ludicrous, to balance things out."

"Which is perfect. The something-ludicrous idea, not the yachting. God, that sounds miserable. If you're going to shoot for something completely off the wall… write our story and sell it to Hollywood." Gavin wasn't sure where the idea came from, but as it bounded into his head, it was obvious and perfect.

"So first"—Aaron mimicked Gavin's tone— "you know it doesn't work that way. And second, where the fuck did that come from?"

The back and forth and the joking were as perfect as everything else about the day. "You miss the con, right? The game. The thrill. The challenge."

"But not the cheating people out of their money."

"No, not that." Gavin shook his head. "But weaving a compelling story. Getting the details right. Sucking someone in and making them believe."

Aaron shrugged, but he was smiling. "Yeah. I do like that bit."

"So—and don't shut me down until you've heard me out—I talked to an agent who's dying to put me in front of someone who would make our movie."

"*Your* movie," Aaron said.

"No, because it's not my story, it's ours. I'm not interested in working with her. Fuck playing myself or how popular I was for another fifteen minutes, a month ago. That life made me miserable. But you thrive on it—being the center of attention while you build the perfect tale. And I can put you in touch with this woman."

The joy on Aaron's face slipped. "Which has me riding your coattails, which is part of what got us here last time—me stepping into shoes that were yours to fill."

"This isn't the same." Gavin fumbled for the right words. "You'd still be the one to write it. Pitch it. Sell it. All I would do is get you that meeting. You try it, and if you get in and like it, you keep doing it. If it's not *all of the above*, you walk away and try something else."

"You make it sound easy."

"It's not. Hard work and all that."

"I have to think about it. But I'm leaning toward *yes*." Aaron's smile was back. "Who do you want to play you?"

Gavin hadn't thought that far. "Uh… Andrew

Garfield?"

Aaron wrinkled his nose.

"What?" Gavin asked through his laugh.

"Nothing, but... I was thinking George Clooney."

"He's almost twenty-five years older than me. And the story Hollywood wants took place nearly a decade ago."

Aaron shrugged. "He's sexy."

Gavin couldn't argue that. "When you decide you're ready, tell me."

"Fuck it. The worst that can happen is someone tells me *no* somewhere along the way. Hook me up."

"I'll put the call in, first thing in the morning. Do you think they can get Emma Watson to play Cynthia?" God damn it, why did he say that? So much for distracting himself. "I don't know where that came from. Never mind."

"I think we'll be lucky to see the cast list before filming starts. There's little to no chance we'll have a say in who's on it. Besides, she's not part of that story." Aaron sighed. "Or this one."

Which was Gavin's cue to drop the subject. "What if she were?" Why couldn't he keep his mouth shut?

"We said no more open relationship. And she's made her feelings pretty clear on the subject." A shadow of hurt reflected in Aaron's eyes.

Right. She didn't like being a third wheel or a fuckdoll. Gavin didn't blame her for that. "Yeah. I shouldn't have said it. Habit." *Or something*. The problem was, now he'd given the thought a voice, it wouldn't shut up. He didn't see her as a one-night stand or a fling. He needed Aaron in his life. He didn't question that, and he'd drop the subject, based on his partner's reaction. But Cynthia was more. Gavin didn't want to relegate their relationship to the occasional passing smile and nothing else. Friendship would be fantastic. More would be better, but only if everyone agreed.

And how dim was he, for bringing that up so soon after getting things back on track with Aaron.

"I get it," Aaron said. "I miss her too, and I see her on a regular basis. I wouldn't mind—fuck it, I'd be happy—if she were a full-time, romantic, equal part of our lives."

Gavin couldn't have put it better. "How selfish of me is it to want to ask her?"

Aaron chuckled.

Gavin looked at him, puzzled. "Not the response I expected. Use your words."

"The laugh is relief that you feel the same way I do. Once again, though, she's made her position pretty clear."

"She doesn't know there's an alternative."

Aaron twisted his mouth in thought. "She might still say *no*."

"I'm prepared for that." Gavin wasn't, really, but he'd accept it. "What are we thinking about?"

"Asking if she wants to be a part of our lives. A lover, not just a business partner or friend."

Gavin liked the sound of that. "Then you're inviting her over for dinner? Something intimate and quiet, the three of us, to propose?"

"Not the word I would use." Aaron raised his

brows. "But appropriate."

As long as it works in practice. Gavin tried to brace himself for things to not go according to his hopes, but he couldn't talk himself out of it. Excitement simmered inside, along with a prayer that Cynthia wouldn't turn them down.

CHAPTER TWENTY-SEVEN

Cynthia felt like it had been weeks since her head was screwed on straight. Two days ago, when Aaron called and invited her over for dinner, it made perfect sense to tell him *no thank you*.

Well, her brain said it made sense. Her heart twisted in on itself, to prevent her from turning him down. The internal struggle was real and frustrating. She was keeping her distance because they'd hurt her. Aaron with the way he acted around Nathan, and Gavin with the assumptions he made about their physical relationship.

But if she was just a business partner, she should be treating things the way she insisted to Aaron she was. She shouldn't care.

She stopped in front of their condo and steeled herself before knocking. It took a while, but Cynthia figured out what nagged her about the call with Emily. *Forgiveness*. Emily gave her a second chance, and what Cynthia held against the guys wasn't even as bad as what she'd done. Holding a grudge would lead to loneliness, knowing she'd walked away from something without trying. She couldn't define it, but it was bigger than she wanted to admit, and it went beyond existing on the fringes of life and watching while other people lived.

The door *snicked* open, and Gavin stood in front of her, wearing a grin that dove past her doubt and buoyed giddiness and hope. "Wonderful surprise," he said.

"Thanks." Her brain ground to a halt. She was supposed to say more. What was it, and why did his cheerful greeting flutter behind her ribs?

He stepped aside. "Come on in."

"Did I forget to send you something?" Aaron asked from his spot on the couch. His smile was more guarded, but she liked seeing it as much as Gavin's.

Right. That was what she was here for. She turned to Gavin. "Actually, I was hoping to talk to you. About business." She'd failed to find a developer, and every time she tried to figure out where to look next, his name popped into her head. She didn't even know if he was still doing work like that. If he was, and he gave her a chance, it wasn't as though she was settling. From what she'd seen, based on the product he created and sold, that made them billionaires, he could have coded circles around her at one point.

"Sure. Do you want to use the office?" Gavin nodded down the hall.

"Here is fine." Technically, a phone call would have been fine, but she missed them both. The job offer was sincere, but also an excuse to visit. "I need a developer, and I was wondering if you'd consid—"

"Yes."

A giggle slipped out before she could stop it,

at his enthusiastic response. "You haven't heard my pitch yet."

"To work for you?" Gavin asked. "On the app? Because I've got an in with a guy who tells me that position is still open, and at the risk of looking desperate, I'd love to slide my fingers into your code and tickle things a little."

With anyone else, she'd question if the innuendo was intentional. The sparkle in Gavin's eye, plus experience, told her of course it was. "Then, um… yay. I'll send over a contract for you to look at, and you can make sure you're okay with the terms."

"Wait. That's it? Conversation over?" Aaron asked.

She shrugged. "I thought it would take more convincing. My pitch has been preempted."

Aaron joined them. "There's still a dinner invitation outstanding if you don't have any plans." When he wrapped an arm around Gavin's waist, the fluttering inside Cynthia scurried away.

She swallowed the reaction. Apparently it was going to take some time to get past whatever that was. Jealousy? Maybe. But not because they had each other. She liked seeing them together and happy. If there was any envy, it was her wanting what they had and she didn't. "I don't think that's a good idea. It sets a precedent I don't want."

"Eating does?" Teasing lined Gavin's question.

And for some reason, that made the ache inside grow. "Don't. Please?"

He furrowed his brow. "Don't… what?"

"Don't do that thing where you talk in circles

and go off on tangents and suck me in, and turn my words back on me until we're so far off the subject, it might as well be in a different universe."

"That's not—"

"It is." And, God help her, she wanted to fall into it.

Aaron gestured to the couch. "Forget dinner, then. He heard you out. Stay long enough to do the same for us?"

She crossed her arms. "I can listen from here. Thank you."

"But you're not. Listening, that is." Gavin rested a palm at the small of her back and nudged her further into the room.

She wanted to sink into the gesture. To focus on how good the spark and warmth felt, searing through her shirt. The need snapped inside, freeing raw confusion and setting loose feelings she thought she'd dealt with. "You're right. I'm not. Because the last time I offered either of you my friendship, you"—she looked at Aaron—"pushed me aside at the end of the night so you could suck face with a stranger, to ignore your misery." She turned to Gavin. "And you tried to use me as a fuck toy, to drown out your pain."

She snapped her jaw shut, and dug deep to find calm. "I shouldn't have said that. And it's another reason I can't stay."

"You meant it, though." Gavin moved back to stand next to Aaron. "And you have every right to be upset."

"We're both sorry," Aaron said.

'I know you are. I heard it the first ten times

you told me. That's fine. I'll get over it. But I'm not going to let it happen again." That was why she was here, though—to repair the bond she shared with them. It hurt when she thought about it. Ached from her toes to her fingertips. "I'm happy you're making things better between you. But I'm not—"

Gavin studied her, sympathy and apology in his eyes. "Not what?"

She shook her head. "You don't get to know that." That she wanted to be a part of what they had. That she hated being so close but not able to touch it.

"I'll go first, then." Gavin grasped her fingers, led her to the couch, and prompted her to sit. He knelt at her feet, never letting go of her hand. "If you don't like what I have to say, you can tell me to go to hell, and I'll accept that and look for the ferryman."

She wanted to tell him *no*, but that fucking hope clawed at her insides again, stealing her words.

"I'm sorry for what I did to you." Gavin held her gaze. "I wasn't… All right, at the time I would have used you. I didn't see it that way because I can't see my life—our lives—without you. That's a lousy excuse for treating you the way I did, but that afternoon at the center, I wasn't thinking of it as a throw-away moment, because in my head, you were already a part of us. Which was an assumption I should have put more thought into, but I couldn't picture the alternative, so I didn't consider there was one."

"In other words, you thought you'd make up with Aaron and I'd be there at your beck and call, for random playtime, when things got back to normal?"

Cynthia meant the question to be flat, but bitterness lined her tone.

"No. Nothing like that." Aaron sat next to her, keeping some distance between them. Those few inches felt like a gaping chasm. "We don't want you as some sort of side dish. We want this to be an equal, three-way relationship. The kind of thing where you're part of our lives and us."

Cynthia swore her heart was breaking and swelling at the same time, and she didn't know how to reconcile the two feelings. How did they go from an apology to this?

"But only if you want the same thing," Gavin said.

"Thanks for taking my opinion into consideration." Sarcasm filled her voice. She didn't want to sound upset, but the walls she'd built to keep them out didn't want to be broken down.

Gavin smiled. "Always. If you say you're not interested in a three-way relationship, we respect that. I love you. Aaron loves you. We hope you feel the same. But if you don't…"

"Of course I do." The words tore free without her permission, rocking inside her with how true they were. "I love you both, and it fucking hurts to hide it, God damn it."

Gavin rose and kissed her. A brush of the lips, so soft, she leaned in for more. He chuckled and nipped at her bottom lip. Something inside her shattered, and she expected the ache to be worse, but instead, it vanished. Her heart soared.

"Now, will you stay for dinner?" Aaron gripped her hand and kissed her fingertips.

She nodded. "What are we having?" Her question came out husky.

Gavin moved to sit on her other side. He drew his lips along her ear, and pleasant chills raced down her spine. "You," he whispered.

It was a simple word, but it sent her pulse screaming through her veins and need dancing over her skin. "I didn't realize I was on the menu."

"Aren't you?" Aaron asked.

"Okay." A girl could get addicted to this kind of attention. Fortunately, it seemed she wasn't the only one who wanted that. "What did you have in mind?"

Gavin settled a palm on her cheek, turning her face to him, and kissed her. When she parted her mouth, he slid his tongue along her bottom lip, then inside. Aaron moved her hair aside and nipped the back of her neck. This was better than sex, and they were barely making out on the couch. But the intimacy of it—the security and promise in each touch and caress—lit up her senses.

Gavin broke away to look her in the eye, forcing her to focus on him despite the series of licks Aaron trailed along her jaw and ear. "I want to watch the two of you finish what I interrupted at the club," Gavin said.

Cynthia hesitated at the nudge of memory. A bitter end to a night that started off so well. "You remember that?"

"It's a curse. I don't forget any of it. Awesome string of learning experiences, though." He grinned. "But onto better things. Is that a *yes*?" He stood and pulled her to her feet.

"Sure."

Aaron gripped her hips and pressed against her back. His erection dug into her ass. "Don't sound so enthusiastic," he teased.

She smirked. "I'm saving the moans of excitement and ecstasy for the bedroom."

"Are you?" Gavin worked his fingers down the front of her blouse, undoing buttons along the way.

Aaron glided his hands up her bare stomach when her shirt fell open. He cupped her breasts and teased her nipples through fabric, tracing light circles, then closing in to pinch and tug.

She groaned and leaned back into him. "Or there are plenty of happy sounds to go around," she managed. When she stepped out of her shoes and kicked them away, she shrank a few inches. Aaron unclasped her bra and slid that and her shirt down her shoulders, to fall at her feet. When his hands met her bare skin, fresh desire spilled in her gut and traveled lower, to pool between her legs.

He took her hand and spun her to face him. He tangled his fingers in her hair and held her head captive, to claim her mouth. She needed more. To be closer. She lost track of who stripped off what in the blur of limbs and kisses and clothes falling away, until she molded her nude body to Aaron's, marveling at the intensity of skin-on-skin contact.

He nipped at her bottom lip, teasing, following the line until he kissed her hard and hungrily. Gavin slid against her back, moving his hands up her chest when she broke the kiss with Aaron.

Gavin sought out the raised nubs on her breasts and rolled them between his fingers, as he sucked on the sensitive skin where her shoulder met her neck.

Aaron slipped his fingers between her legs, sliding easily along her slit. He held her gaze while he honed in on her clit, and she couldn't hold back her whimper. It wasn't just the physical sensations pushing her toward climax. The *who* was as arousing as what they did to her. The moment was more real and more ethereal than anything she'd experienced before. It tugged at her soul and crushed her doubt.

She was safe here. And desired. And she would offer them both the same in return. It was all perfect.

CHAPTER TWENTY-EIGHT

The combination of Aaron stroking her and Gavin pinching and kissing pulled Cynthia to the edge, but didn't tip her over. When Gavin bit her shoulder, the sharp sting sent her spiraling into climax. She bucked her hips, not sure if she wanted to be closer to Aaron's touch or pull away from it. Her head swam, like it might float away.

As orgasm ebbed, her legs felt like rubber bands, and she was grateful both men held her upright.

Aaron wrapped an arm around her waist and lowered his mouth to her ear. "Now you can use whatever you were saving for the bedroom."

Cynthia's chuckle was weak, but she looked forward to what came next. She let herself be led down the hall, and Aaron lowered her onto the bed. He leaned over her to grab a condom from the nightstand drawer, and rolled it on.

When he nudged her opening with the head of his cock, she thrust her hips toward him, and he inched back with a smirk. He brushed a strand of hair from her face. "I'm memorizing the moment. How incredible you look. How amazing this all is."

"All right." A new wave of heat flushed her skin.

He eased into her an inch at a time, spreading her and drawing a long moan. When he was buried to the hilt, he slid out just as slowly, then entered her again. She didn't know if she wanted to beg him to hurry or savor the slow build that tingled in her nerves.

The mattress shifted with the weight of a new body, and Gavin knelt next to her. He'd shed his clothes as well. He lowered his head to her nipple and sucked hard. The contrast in sensations between her legs and her chest jolted new senses to life. He worked his hand lower, to tease her sensitive clit, not letting up on his attention to her chest.

She reached for Gavin, needing something to grip. Wanting *more*. How was that possible with so much already going on? She found his shaft and stroked. His groan vibrating against her skin was as enticing as his touch.

Each time Aaron thrust deep inside her, he struck something, and her body pinged with need.

Cynthia pulled Gavin's mouth to hers, feeling greedy and not at all bad about it. She kissed him, branding the moment into her mind. "I want to taste you," she said.

He gave her the cocky grin she adored, and moved to kneel next to her head. He fisted his cock and stroked, and she flicked out her tongue to glide along the head and rod.

"*Fuck*. You're gorgeous, Cyn." Aaron's voice was strained.

She felt more dirty than anything, but in all

the best ways. Orgasm lunged forward this time, not dragging out, and she screamed when she came, clenching around Aaron's cock. He continued to pound into her. She clenched the sheets in her fists until her knuckles ached, and rode the climax that tore through her.

Through the haze that fogged her thoughts, she heard Gavin grunt. A moment later, sticky, wet fluid spurted across her face and chest.

Aaron gripped her thighs, slamming against her in stuttered bursts. Despite the condom, she swore she felt him spill inside. He continued to hammer for several seconds, before he slowed to a stop.

This wasn't just perfect. If there was a word that meant better than perfect, it described now. This arrangement. This pocket of belonging she'd discovered.

After she cleaned up, Cynthia lay in bed next to Gavin, Aaron on his other side. She could stay in this moment forever, even if that wasn't at all practical or realistic. But she didn't think she'd be forgetting it any time soon.

"I really do love you both," she murmured against Gavin's chest. She raised her head enough to look him in the eye. "And if you say *I know*, I'll…" She trailed off, not sure what kind of threat she could make.

"I don't have to. You said it for me."

She looked at Aaron, who was watching the exchange. "You don't have anything to add?" she asked in a teasing tone.

*

"Now that you're here, settled, and comfortable, you're staying for a while, I assume," Aaron said.

He lay on his back, head on Gavin's arm. Cynthia was on Gavin's other side, curled up against him. If Aaron had seen Cyn this comfortable with Gavin a month ago, when she was *just a fling*, he would have wondered what she had that Aaron didn't. Now, he didn't want to take her place; he needed *her* here. He loved Gavin completely, but Cynthia offered a new type of balance and stability. One he didn't want to imagine going without.

Cynthia arched her brows. "*A while* is a bit vague. Are you thinking one hour? Four? Overnight?"

"All of the hours." Gavin kissed her forehead, and she lay down again.

"I was going to start with *the weekend.*" Aaron paused, as Gavin's suggestion settled into his head and refused to budge. "But now that he mentioned it…"

Cynthia reached across Gavin's chest to tangle her fingers with Aaron's. "I *am* getting sick of the view from my motel room."

"*Sick of the view.* Perfect reason to leave it behind and move in with a couple of random guys." Aaron kept the teasing in his words.

She laughed. "Random? Yeah, I suppose that's accurate, but not the way you're implying. I meant what I said a few weeks ago. There's something between us—all of us—that makes me feel like I've known you forever. It's pleasant."

"Bah." Gavin spat out the sound. "*Pleasant* is such a tame word. Limp. Weak. Seventy-degree weather with a light breeze is pleasant. Vanilla ice cream is pleasant. You, my dear, and this entire affair, are fucking incredible."

Aaron sat so he could see them both better. "I have to agree with that. And the suggestion of having you here full time. So, yeah. Move in with us?"

"I don't know." Despite her sigh and flat expression, mischief danced in Cynthia's eyes. "I mean, what if hiring Gavin doesn't work out? Then I'll have to replace him. Things will be awkward at home, and you'll both resent me."

Gavin snorted. "You're not going to find *anyone* better than me. But it doesn't matter, because if that's what's holding you back, I won't take the job in the first place."

"I promise I was kidding." Cynthia's pleading tone cracked, and she giggled. "I'm done pretending at this point that I can keep work separate from the two of you, but it doesn't matter. I want to be in your lives. So yes. I'd love to live here with you."

"Of course you would." Gavin was smug.

Aaron shook his head. "What he means to say is, *Thank God.* Because it wouldn't feel right any other way." He leaned over Gavin, to kiss Cyn. Warmth and completeness danced over Aaron's skin. He never in a thousand years would have crafted a story that ended like this, because it was too implausible. But it was also exactly what he wanted. Gavin, Cynthia—they were what he wanted in his life. They could deal with the rest, however it worked out, as long as he had them.

EPILOGUE

NINE MONTHS LATER

Gavin's pulse hammered in his ears, and his heart lodged in his throat at the sight of the red carpet. The fans lining it. The stars strolling down. It had been years since he stepped foot on something like that. It was a silly thing, when he forced himself to think about it. A cheap, temporary piece of rug, special only because of its color and location.

He didn't understand why this movie was getting so much fanfare, for a premier screening. Aaron's agent insisted—multiple times—this was bigger than Gavin wanted to admit. Huge enough that, once a studio had the screenplay, they fast-tracked casting and production to get the movie out there while there was still buzz around it.

"Hey. You all right?" Aaron's question dragged Gavin's attention back to the inside of the car. Aaron reached across the aisle of the back seat and squeezed his hand.

Gavin nodded. "Glad I'm not out there." He looked at Cynthia, whose wide-eyed gaze was fixed through the window.

"So many people." Awe filled her voice. "To

see a movie about the two of you." She looked stunning in a blue evening dress that matched her eyes and hugged her figure. She'd fit in on the carpet.

"Eh." Gavin kissed her bare shoulder. "Maybe sixty percent about us. I hear from a reliable source that the rest is utter fiction."

The driver inched along with traffic. When he rounded the corner and the crowds dipped into the background, Gavin managed to grasp a sense of calm again. He might be coping better with his response to the crowds these days, but he wasn't ready to test his resolve by diving into the middle of it.

Fortunately, since the invitation to the screening was Aaron's, and most of the cameras and fans were there for the actors, the three got to skip the fanfare out front and slip into the theater through the back entrance. Technically, Gavin and Cynthia could have dressed down and blended in better. However, Cynthia was so excited to attend an actual Hollywood premier, he insisted they go all out, appearance-wise.

A moment later, they stepped from the car. No one was back here except drivers parking in rows of black, shiny, luxury cars. Gavin wrapped an arm around Cynthia's waist, intertwined his fingers with Aaron's, and led them inside. An usher seated them near the front, on the outside aisle.

For the next hour or so, they watched everyone else trickle in and take their seats.

Aaron's agent negotiated an almost unheard-of deal, getting Aaron a say in the revision process and putting him on set during filming. Which meant Gavin and Cynthia had met most of the cast and crew as well. Unknown actors were cast in the lead roles, and Gavin was great with that. He was only mildly surprised to find out they were fans. His shock came in discovering they still admired him after reading the screenplay.

The theater lights flickered, and the director stepped in front of the screen, to a round of applause. He waited until the noise died down. "Evening, everyone. Thank you for coming. I was prompted to say a few words, but I'm not going to use all my time, because I'm not the reason you're here. We're fortunate enough to have in our audience tonight, two people who lived this story."

Gavin's stomach dropped into his shoes, and his mouth went dry.

"So tonight"—the director continued, blissfully unaware of the impact his words were having—"I want to introduce you to Aaron Birch, the screenplay writer and one of the key reasons we're able to bring you this movie."

The tension in Gavin's neck evaporated, and he clapped Aaron on the back when his partner stood. Aaron gave him a sheepish smile, before making his way to the stage.

"I didn't expect that," Aaron said with a confident laugh. He looked at ease in front of the crowd, as if working a room of Hollywood's finest came naturally.

It would have to, given how Aaron earned his livelihood in his mid- and late-teens. Cynthia squeezed Gavin's hand, and he gripped back.

"I don't have much to say." Aaron's tone never wavered. It carried through the room, firm and strong. "I wouldn't have survived the past without my amazing partner. Hands off, ladies and gentlemen. Gavin Jackson is mine." Light laughter rippled through the crowd. "And I wouldn't be up here now, without the loves of my life."

Warmth filled Gavin, starting in his chest and spreading through every inch of him. He'd never seen Aaron happier with a job. But this was a career; already Aaron had multiple offers on the table. It wasn't a surprise to Gavin that Aaron had a knack for making fiction more plausible than reality, which gave him his pick of writing jobs.

"And that's it from me. Enjoy the show." Aaron stepped back into the aisle, and the lights dimmed. The room was dark, and the opening strains of the score filled the air when he made it back to their seats.

He kissed Cynthia and Gavin, before taking his own spot again.

It was strange, watching their teenage years unfold on the big screen. Gavin had seen himself on camera more times than he could count, but now it was someone else as him. There were moments he wanted to shout, *That's not how it happened.* He understood why Aaron, the director, and the producer, made the choices they did in alterations, but it was still surreal.

Watching actor-him go through one phase of addiction and seeing actor-Aaron's response from the outside gnawed at Gavin. And there was a fresh surge of bitterness that the movie ended with the four-billion-dollar deal, all those years ago, wrapping things up as if that were the *happily ever after*, instead of just a stop-gap.

"You all right?" This time it was Cynthia asking.

He swallowed the bile of the past and nodded. "You sure you don't want to go to the after party?" he whispered in her ear.

"I'm sure. Besides, we have work in the morning."

Gratitude whispered through him. He tugged Aaron's hand, and the three slipped out as the closing credits rolled.

As the car took them home, Gavin couldn't stop himself from sliding into the past—memories of how things really went, the thrill of falling in love, the rush of pulling off the biggest tech sale of its time, the highs and lows that led them here...

Aaron and Cynthia involved him in the conversation, but after a few single-syllable responses, they left him alone.

They arrived at the condo building, and Gavin tried to pull himself back to the present on the elevator ride upstairs. The haze still clouded his mind, movie-facts overlapping reality.

They made it inside the house, and Aaron stepped in front of him to loosen Gavin's tie. "You coming back to us anytime tonight? You can stay wherever you are, but I promise here is better."

Something about Aaron's comment—the words, the sympathy mixed with teasing, or all of it—snapped Gavin out of the fog of the past. He smiled, as a sense of peace flowed through him, and he brushed his lips over Aaron's. "You're right. It is," he said.

"That was different. The crowds, not the film." Cynthia shrank three inches when she stepped from her heels. "Though the movie was one of a kind as well." She looked at Gavin. "Don't ever feel obligated to do a red carpet event again, just to sate my curiosity."

His amusement spilled out in a laugh. "You had to do it once, so you could say you did. Otherwise, you'd wonder forever if you missed out on something big."

"I guess." She turned away.

Gavin grabbed her wrist and spun her back to face him. Cupping her cheeks, he kissed her deeply. "Tell me you won't share every little detail with Emily," he said when they broke apart.

She grinned. "Totally will. But that doesn't mean I want to do it again."

He dropped onto the couch, not caring what it would do to his tux, and calmness took root. A year ago, this simple teasing would have been an act on his part. A night like tonight would have jarred him into a place it would take days to crawl out of, and the tension never really faded.

Tonight it was all genuine. He didn't feel like he had to act a certain way. He watched Aaron uncork a bottle of chilled, sparkling grape juice, and Cynthia grabbed cupcakes from the kitchen. She'd ordered a batch with marzipan screenplays on top, because she insisted this was celebration-worthy.

Gavin agreed. Then again, he thought the entire arrangement—the three of them, the love and respect that flowed between them—was all celebration-worthy. This was better than a

Hollywood *happily ever after*. It was real. It was intense. He got to share the adoration of the two most amazing people in the universe. And he wouldn't have things any other way.

ABOUT ALLYSON LINDT

ALLYSON LINDT IS A FULL-TIME GEEK and a fuller-time contemporary romance author. She likes her stories with sweet geekiness and heavy spice, because cubicle dwellers need love too. She loves a sexy happily-ever-after and helping deserving cubicle dwellers find their futures together.